WHO'S A GOOD BOY?

A STORY OF RESCUED LOVE

LEXXIE COUPER

Who's A GOOD BOY?

A dog trainer, a single dad, a three-legged dog, and rescued love...

LEXXIE COUPER

DEDICATION

For everyone who's ever welcomed a rescued dog into their home and hearts.

And for Ebony, my own rescued dog who changed everything for our family for the better.

WHO'S A GOOD BOY?

1

Tim

SNAGGING a pink tutu-wearing teddy bear up off the hallway floor without slowing down, I toss it through the closest open door and then head for the kitchen. "Ellie, we're going to be late!" I call over my shoulder.

Coffee. I need coffee. A bucket of coffee. Maybe a trough.

Ellie, wherever she is in the apartment, deigns not to answer.

"Ellie?" I call again, this time snagging up my car keys from where I'd tossed them onto the counter the night before. I bounce them on my palm, looking around the kitchen. God, I hope I remembered to charge the car last night. If I'm late for this interview...

Maybe I *should* have accepted the invite to use Dad's driver.

A shudder ripples through me.

Nope. Not an option. I'd promised myself if I was doing this

—moving away from the academic life into the political one—I wasn't going to ride Dad's coattails. What message would that send?

That you're a Holt through and through?

"Ellie? Are you coming?" Maybe I should change my surname? "Hello," I mutter under my breath, extending my hand to an imaginary constituent standing in front of me. "I'm Timothy Fartybutt, Prime Minister of Australia."

A wry snort vibrates at the back of my nose. Ellie would be impressed.

Speaking of which... "Ellie? Hurry up!"

From deep in the interior of the apartment, a toilet flushes.

Ah, okay. That explains it.

The sound of feet thumping along polished bamboo flooring precedes the sudden arrival of a tornado dressed in pink tulle, faded denim, and a colour that could only be called cat-vomit yellow. On a good day. "Where's Lord Byron?" Ellie asks, wildly looking around the kitchen. Her pigtails are a lopsided mess of strawberry-blond frizz, fixed with mismatched scrunchies.

No way in hell am I going to suggest I fix them though. Never mess with a seven-year-old's hair when she's done it herself. I learnt that the hard way a month ago.

"Byron is in your bedroom," I say, jogging/shuffling on the spot. "We're late. C'mon. Let's go. Let's go."

"In my *bedroom*?" Her eyes grow wider. "*Daddy*."

She pivots on her hot-pink Vans and bolts back into the apartment.

I groan.

Yep. Definitely going to be late.

As if fully aware of the situation, my phone springs into life in the hip pocket of my chinos, the ring tone telling me *exactly* who it is.

"Hurry up, Ellie!" I call, tugging my phone free and jamming it to my ear. "What's up, Dad?"

"Where are you?" Robert Holt—once Australia's most beloved Prime Minister, now rabble-rouser antagonist to whomever happened to be the leader of the country at the time—asks.

"Waiting for Byron," I answer.

Dad knows who Byron is and how much the bear is loved by Ellie. The illustrious and revered Robert Holt can very easily be angry with me, his only son and heir apparent, but being angry with his only granddaughter?

Dad sighs. "Colin is outside that shoebox you call an apartment. Hurry up. He'll take you to the studio."

"I don't need Colin, Dad." I claw a hand through my hair. Dad's driver, while a nice guy, is also a consummate spy for Dad.

"Colin is waiting," Dad repeats. "And Lyle is in the car as well."

For fuck's...

I grit my teeth. "Dad, I don't need a minder."

"Lyle is a political publicist, Timothy. The best in the country."

"I don't need one of those, either." I press my phone to my chest and throw a look toward Ellie's room. "Els, hurry up!"

"A forty-two-year-old single-father environmentalist about to make the shift into politics," Dad is saying when I return the phone to my ear. I can only assume the admonition started with *You do when you're.* "Especially," Dad keeps going, "one who's a widower and who's been a tad, how shall I say this? controversial? throughout his academic career."

I grit my teeth again. Harder. Something cracks. Or feels like it does. Well, there goes my upper molar dental crown.

"I'm not controversial," I point out. "I'm honest. If the collective citizens of this planet don't—"

"Your image needs polishing, son, and Lyle—"

"We're here," Ellie crows, bounding into the kitchen. Her pigtails are gone, replaced with a gravity-defying ponytail and a neon-pink cat ears headband. Lord Byron is still dressed in his tutu, but now he has a fat and floppy pink ribbon tied around his neck.

Her timing is perfect.

"I gotta go, Dad." I grin at Ellie, frantically, comically, waving her toward the door. "I'll talk to you after the interview."

"Timoth—"

I kill the connection. Dad is incredible, supportive, and hmm...how should I put this? A tad overbearing?

Snorting, I hurry after Ellie—now yanking open the apartment's door. "Straight to the parking level, Els. No chatting with Mrs. Angelo this morning."

"But she'll be sad if she doesn't get to give me my morning milkshake," Ellie protests, skipping to the lift doors, Byron bouncing against her leg.

"Mrs. Angelo can give you an afternoon milkshake instead." The octogenarian on the second floor decided to give Ellie a "comfort treat" the morning after Belinda passed away and hasn't stopped. That basically equals eighteen months of milkshakes every school morning and some kind of freshly baked pastry every weekend morning. Mrs. Angelo used to make a milkshake for me as well until my belt buckle gave me a lecture.

The weekend pastries, however... Yeah, no way I'm refusing those.

Ellie pulls a face—part disappointment, part anticipation—and jabs the lift's Down button. "Okay. I can wait."

"Thata girl." Smiling, I check my watch and wince. Yeah, ridiculously late. It isn't entirely Ellie's fault though. Since cancer won its hard-fought battle with Belinda, time has been a little more fluid in the Holt household. Especially mornings. They kind of creep up on me in surprise attacks of disoriented emptiness.

I'd thrown myself into work—I may not have been able to save my wife, but if I work hard enough, I might be able to save the world—and thrown myself harder into being the best dad I can be.

The best dad I can be is, invariably, prone to running late.

Ellie doesn't mind. As long as Lord Byron is with her, she has no relationship with time.

The joys of youth.

"So, what's on the program for this afternoon?" I ask as we wait for the lift to arrive. "Karate?"

"That's tomorrow," Ellie points out, adjusting her school backpack on her shoulder. She smiles up at me and as always, my heart squeezes. I love her more than breath. "Today's ballet."

I arch a playful eyebrow. "Since when do you do ballet?"

Ellie giggles. Belinda had been a professional ballerina for the Australian Ballet Company, and Ellie is definitely following in her mother's footsteps. "Daddy."

I pull a confused face. "I thought you did—"

The lift doors open, the man occupying the interior killing my intended joke about Ellie doing plumbing classes.

I don't hide my groan. "Good morning, Lyle."

Lyle Asher sighs, holding the door open with one shiny black leather-shod foot. "I'm not the enemy, Timothy." He turns his laser-like focus to Ellie, a smile curling the corners of his lips. "Good morning, Elisabeth. I like your outfit. It's a good look."

"Thanks." Ellie lifts up Byron for inspection. "Do you like—"

"You are going to be late." Lyle snaps his drilling attention back to me. "*Not* a good look. We need to hurry. I'll prep you for the interview on the way."

Grinding my teeth for a third time—damn, I'll need to make a dentist appointment later today—I hold his stare. "We're good. I'll meet you at the studio."

Lyle compresses his lips but bites back the retort he no doubt wants to lob my way.

Ellie steps a little closer to my leg, her shoulder brushing my thigh as she hugs Byron to her chest, her wary eyes on Lyle.

"C'mon, Els," I murmur, scooping her up onto my hip and stepping into the lift. She's too old to do such a thing to—at least, I think she is—but she giggles and clings to me, and I like that a hell of a lot more than cautious uncertainty.

Maybe this political career *is* a bad idea. I want to change the world for my daughter, and all the children out there, I want to help it survive mankind, but at what expense?

"Daddy?" Ellie whispers as I jab the button for the car park five floors down.

Lyle follows us into the lift, letting out a frustrated breath.

I ignore him, beaming at Ellie instead.

"Yes, short stuff?" I haven't called her short stuff for a while, but I'm feeling protective of her. And a little guilty.

Ellie tightens her arms around my shoulders. "Can we get a dog?"

"*Yes!*" Lyle declares. "Getting a dog is actually on my list. It's an ideal move to appeal to the voters we are—"

"Wait, wait, wait," I burst out, at the exact moment Ellie squeals "We *can*? *Yay!*"

"I'm thinking a Cavoodle," Lyle goes on, withdrawing an iPad from the messenger bag hanging from his shoulder. He swipes his thumb over the screen, focus fixed on it. "Or maybe a Shiba Inu. Possibly a Bichon—"

What? What, what, *what*?

"We're *not* getting a dog," I yelp.

Ellie wilts on my hip. "We're not?"

Lyle narrows his eyes at me.

Great. Now *I'm* the bad guy.

Before I can stop her, Ellie wriggles out of my arms and thuds to the lift floor, hugging Lord Byron.

Lyle cocks an eyebrow at me.

Talk about being judged right now.

I scrunch up my face, claw my hands through my hair, and then crouch down in front of Ellie, brushing a strand of strawberry-blond hair from her face. "We live in an apartment, Els," I point out softly. "Where would the dog hang out when we are at work and school?"

"My bedroom," she mumbles. This is not the first conversation about getting a dog we've had. She made a PowerPoint presentation about getting one two months ago, complete with poll results she'd conducted at her school. Who would have thought ten seven-year-olds—and Mrs. Crumpton, for some reason—would all agree we needed a dog?

Before I can respond, the lift doors chime and open, revealing our apartment building's entry lobby. Not the underground parking level.

I flick Lyle an exasperated look.

"Oops." He shrugs, not a hint of contrition on his face. "But seeing as we're here, look, there's Colin."

Sure enough, sitting directly outside the building's main doorway, is a black Audi SUV.

I bite back a muttered curse as Colin appears from the driver's side, and—smile wide—places a McDonald's milkshake on the Audi's roof before finger-gunning at Ellie.

"Milkshake!" Ellie shouts, running from the lift.

"I'm going to bloody kill you, Dad," I mutter, rising to my feet. Of course, the ex-leader of the country knows exactly how to bribe his granddaughter.

"It wasn't your father who organised the milkshake," Lyle says over his shoulder as he strides from the lift after Ellie. "This is why you need me."

I sigh. And follow.

Exiting my building, my focus locked on Colin handing Ellie the milkshake, I'm about to say good morning to Dad's driver—or maybe I'm about to suggest bribing a seven-year-old isn't exactly principled—when something slams into me.

Something body-sized and warm and soft and smelling of pineapple.

A damp sensation spreads over my side, the smell of pineapple grows stronger, and I stagger sideways, pinwheeling my arms as I lose my footing. I hear someone say "Crap. What the—", I see Ellie's eyes and mouth grow wide, I see Colin begin to hurry toward me.

See the world tilt completely off its axis.

And then I hit the footpath.

Hard.

Surrounded by the smell of pineapple.

2

C *helsea*

Shit. Shit. Shit. Shit. Shit.

I've collided with someone.

Shit. That's what I get for checking my phone while running—no, sprinting—to avoid a freaking parking ticket.

Argh!

And of course, the pineapple juice I was attempting to drink—my very woeful breakfast—is now spilt.

Double argh!

Shooting the poor sod I've run into a quick look—oh boy, he's covered in juice—I hold out my hand to him. "Sorry."

"Daddy!" A little munchkin with amazing strawberry-blond frizzy curls suddenly appears at his side. "Are you okay?"

I take a step back. The family resemblance is undeniable. The munchkin and the guy on the footpath both have light-blue eyes and red hair, although his hair is a deep auburn red, not the fair copper of his daughter.

Huh, he's cute. Really cute.

Maybe I should introduce myself?

Hi, I'm Chelsea Parker. Your friendly neighbourhood—

"Are you okay, sir?" An older gentleman arrives on the scene, carrying a brightly coloured milkshake container.

Frowning, I take another step back. Wow, the people of Balmain really take their fallen pedestrians seriously.

I look back at the insanely cute guy on the footpath. "I'm so sorry," I say, holding out my hand again as I step towards him. "I really wasn't—"

"What the actual hell?" An immaculately dressed man who looks maybe twenty-five, maybe thirty-five, charges up to the other man's side, his glare locking on me. "Why don't you watch where you're going?"

I blink. I don't do conflict, but whoa, way to ignite the fire. If I were a dog, I'd bare my teeth.

Instead, I straighten a little, and play with the straw of the glass bottle once full of pineapple juice. Projecting calm and zero threat. "I didn't mean to—"

"No, no." The guy I ran into shoves himself to his feet and brushes off his butt, chuckling as the little munchkin helps. "I'm okay."

Retreating a step, all too aware I'm still the recipient of a hostile glare, I give him a narrowed-eyed look. Now that he's upright, he looks familiar. "Do I know you?"

Chelsea! Parking ticket! Next client! Move!

"Everyone knows Daddy," the munchkin declares. "He's—"

"Running late," he cuts in, pressing his palm gently over her mouth with a laugh. He smiles at me, and my heart does a weird little flutter. He's not just cute, he's freaking here-take-my-panties hot. "Sorry to just walk out in front of you like that," he continues, eyes twinkling as his smile stretches. My insides melt. Take-my-panties-and-my-bra hot. "I should have looked."

"You *should* be going," the man of the ambiguous age interjects. "*We* need to be going. Now."

He shoots daggers at me with his eyes. Agitation and possessiveness rolls off him.

Whoa.

"Relax, Lyle," the still familiar, still insanely cute guy says.

The glaring Lyle bunches his perfectly shaved jaw. "I'm relaxed. But we are late."

I ignore Lyle, checking out the guy I knocked over instead. A small part of me recognises he's holding my gaze. Actually holding it. Wow. I mean, seriously, wow. He's cute and he's holding my gaze. Another small part acknowledges the fact I'm enjoying the hell out of it.

I don't do conflict and I don't do flirting, but he's looking at me and he's cute and...

See where it goes, Chelsea. Go on. Have some fun. You can't spend your life only focused on—

"We're late," Lyle announces, as if I didn't hear him the first time. I can almost see his hackles rising, destroying the perfect comb-back of his slick black hair.

My hair has never been a perfect anything. God, did I even do it this morning? I try to remember. Nope, no clue.

Let's hope the curls hide the possible absence of a brush. Maybe everyone will think I've just got a really expensive beach hairdo.

I clear my throat, struggling not to reach up and touch my hair. "I need to go as well," I say, looking at the very cute, very familiar guy.

His gaze grabs mine again, and yep, he's definitely holding it. "Sorry for getting in your road," he says.

"Anytime." I let my lips curl into a smile as I turn away. "Sorry for knocking you off your feet," I finish over my shoulder.

I'm flirting. I'm actually flirting. Go me!

"Anytime," he calls after me.

And he's flirting with me. I think. Is he? He is, right? Oh God, why am I so bad at this?

Because you suck at dealing with humans, Chelsea. Suck, suck, suck.

His daughter waves at me, and I wave back. And grin. At him. At the delicious little butterflies-flutter his playful compliment stirs in my stomach.

Maybe I don't suck at dealing with humans? Maybe I'm better at it than I thought. A year after being dumped by Roger —the only serious relationship I'd ever had—a year after many failed first dates and aborted Tinder interactions, I'd begun to believe I was.

But perhaps this serendipitous moment with the familiar stranger is proving Roger wrong.

Perhaps?

Okay, maybe I'm putting the cart before the horse. One little flirtatious interaction and one brief second of eye-contact does not a femme fatale make. But still, when was the last time a living creature apart from an animal has made me grin?

Because I can't help myself, I shoot a look back over my shoulder.

He's watching me, poised to climb into the backseat of a black Audi SUV, the older gentleman who'd asked if he was okay holding the door open for him.

Holding the door for him? What the?

Who the hell is this guy? A celebrity of some sort? Is that why he looks familiar?

He smiles at me.

Before I know it, I smile back.

And then, with a small wave, he disappears into the backseat of the Audi.

A thick sense of loss ripples through me and I let out a sigh. "Yep. Missed opportunity right there."

The older gentleman closes the door, pins me with a contemplative scrutiny I feel all the way to my spine, and then strides around to the driver's door.

Lyle and the cutie-pie munchkin are nowhere to be seen. In the car already, no doubt.

I chew my bottom lip. With the possessive way Lyle kept glaring at me, it's probably better it's all over but the singing.

Still, damn, he was cute. The guy I knocked over. Not Lyle.

Turning, I hurry to where I parked my car earlier in the morning. Sprint to it, in fact. As fun as the interlude has been, I'm going to be quite late to my next client. Brutus won't care. As long as I come with liver treats—which I always do—the Rottie with a phobia of skateboarders will be happy to see me no matter how late I am. His owner however, Marjory Whitton, well, she will mind very much.

Marjory isn't someone to irritate. The twenty-seven-year-old social media influencer with her 1.8 million faithful followers can make or break a small business like mine.

There is a glut of dog trainers in Sydney, but only a few who a/ specialise in helping dogs with anxiety and social disorders, and b/ have celebrity clients.

The first time Marjory posted about Oh Behave Dog Training, I was flooded with new clients—case in point, the one I'd just finished with. That client, a personal trainer who thought Marjory walked on water, had managed to lock herself, her dog, and me—*and* my handbag and car keys and phone—out of her waterfront apartment and not discovered it until the session had finished. Hence why I'm now running late for Marjory's session.

Argh.

Throwing myself into my old but beloved VW Beetle, I check my watch—shit, I'm so late—my windscreen wiper—no, no ticket. Phew—my phone—no text from Marjory demanding to know where I am. Also, phew—and my side mirror.

My heart stops.

Black Audi SUV.

Black Audi SUV.

Black Audi S—

It drives pass me, and for a fleeting second, I glimpse the insanely cute guy I'd knocked over in the backseat.

And for an even fleeting-er second, his eyes meet mine through our side windows.

And then he's gone.

I sit still, gripping my steering wheel. Heart racing. Who *is* he? *Why* does he look so familiar?

Will I ever see him a—

My phone bursts into life on the passenger seat and I let out a little squeal as "Who Let The Dogs Out?" fills the Beetle's interior with crazy gusto and volume.

Yes, I know my ringtone is cliched and corny. No, I don't care.

Trying to get my heart back under some kind of control, I look at my phone's screen. "Great," I groan, my stomach sinking.

Marjory Whitton is calling me.

Damn it.

Ignoring the call, I throw my car into gear and shoot out into the crazy Balmain traffic.

Marjory lives in Woolloomooloo. With this peak-hour morning traffic it's going to take me way too long to get—

"Who Let The Dogs Out?" blasts out of my phone again.

"Shit," I mutter, seeing Marjory's name on its screen. Scrunching my eyes closed for a split second, I connect the call. "Hi, Marjory," I say, as bright and cheery as an overly caffeinated kindergarten teacher. "I'm on my way. Sorry, just got caught up with—"

"Timothy Holt," Marjory exclaims. "I know. When are you going to introduce me to him?"

I frown. "Who?"

"Timothy Holt," she repeats. "I saw a photo of you with him on Instagram just now."

"Instagram?" What on earth is she talking about? "I'm not on Instagram. I've just finished with a client in Balmain, one of your followers, actually, and I'm heading—"

"Yes!" A predatory mix of excitement and impatience fills her voice. I can almost see the same mix on her gorgeous Millennial face. "Balmain. That's where Timothy Holt lives. I want you to introduce me to him. Today."

Something deep in the recesses of my mind itches. Holt. Holt. Why is that name familiar? Maybe I went to school with him? But why would a famous social influencer know him if that's the case? No idea. "Who the hell is Timothy Holt?"

"You're kidding, right?"

Now I can almost see the *shock* on Marjory's face. Can definitely hear it in her voice.

"I don't—"

"The ex-Prime Minister of Australia's son," she declares. "Drop dead gorgeous. Widower. On everyone who's anyone's invite list despite the fact he rarely accepts a single one." She snorts. "And as an aside, also on *my* devour list."

"Your *what*?" I don't speak social influencer. I also don't speak Millennial. If that's what Marjory's speaking.

"So when *are* you going to introduce me to him?" she asks again. Or is it more of a demand?

Flicking on my indicator, I inch my way into a minute gap in the next lane, wave my appreciation at the car now behind me, and then frown. "Marjory, I really don't know what... Wait, you said you saw this photo of me and Timothy Holt just now on Instagram? Who took it?"

"No idea. Some rando. They uploaded it with the hashtag #TimHoltIsHot which I follow just in case he's spotted somewhere near where I am. But it turns out I've had a direct line to him all along."

An itch begins to crawl over my scalp as I picture the insanely cute guy I'd collided with. Good grief, had I really run into Robert Holt's son? "Where *were* we when the photo was taken?"

"A busy footpath. There was you, Timothy, an old dude in a suit, some other guy with a messenger bag—seriously not on trend right now—who was glaring at you, and Timothy's daughter."

My face prickles with heat. Shit. Shit. I knocked over the ex-PM's son. I crashed into the ex-PM of Australia's son.

"You know him, right?" Marjory asks. "The way he's smiling at you, it looks like you're old friends. Not that you're *that* old—what are you? In your forties?"

"I'm thirty-seven," I mumble, my mind replaying over and over every minute, every second of my interaction with Timothy Holt. Did I do anything considered a threat? Apart from knocking him off his feet, of course? Is the old guy his bodyguard? Were the federal police—

"Thirty-seven? Really? Wow, okay, then."

Oh my God, why does she sound so shocked? How old did she think I am?

"Well, Timothy's forty-two," Marjory continues. "Which isn't *that* old, not when *I'm* only in my mid-twenties." She laughs. "So, if you could just introduce me to him, I would love you forever." She pauses. For a beat. "And rave about Oh Behave for another month on all my socials."

The last is dangled like bait.

Of course, I can introduce you to him, Marjory. Damn, wouldn't it be good if I could say that? To actually *personally* know Timothy Holt...

I mean, how good for my *business* would it be to personally know Timothy Holt so I could introduce him to Marjory and get all that influencer magic?

I picture Timothy Holt again. Remember the way he'd smiled at me. The way I'd responded to that smile...

How good would it be to be able to say, *We're as thick as thieves. We have coffee regularly?*

Does he like coffee? Is he a coffee person or a tea person? Does he like movies? Hiking? Gary and I love hiking. Is Timothy a hiking person? Is Timothy a dog person? What *would* Gary think of him? To be fair, my ten-year-old Blue Heeler-Labrador cross loves almost everyone, but I always trust his judgement with those he doesn't love.

A car horn sounds behind me, and I blink. Shit, I'm driving in peak Sydney traffic daydreaming about being in some kind of relationship with the closest thing to Australian royalty there is instead of focusing on the road. What the hell is wrong with me?

For a foolish second, I consider telling Marjory that of *course* I know Timothy Holt. Of *course*, I'll introduce her to him. The influencer would be so impressed that who knows *how* many more clients Oh Behave Dog Training would get during the time between Marjory raving about me on social media and me working out where Timothy Holt was so I could abduct him and convince him to pretend we know each other. Without getting arrested by the federal police, of course.

I snort.

"I don't know Timothy Holt, Marjory," I say instead. "I accidentally bumped into him this morning rushing to my car after seeing a client. So no chance of an introduction. Sorry."

"Hmm." Marjory doesn't sound convinced. Does she think I'm trying to keep the guy all to myself?

Admit it, if you did know him, wouldn't you do just that?

I snort again. Hell yeah, I would.

"I'm on my way," I state, not hiding the wry laughter in my voice. "I hope you haven't fed Brutus this morning."

"Oops." Marjory giggles and my stomach sinks. Here we go. "Sorry. I gave him breakfast fifteen minutes ago. The new brand of kibble I'm endorsing on Instagram arrived this morning, and Brutus was going nuts, and you know me when it comes to him. I can't deny him anything."

I bite back a sigh.

"Oh, by the way," she says, clearly unimpressed with my professional disappointment, "I've just reposted that shot of you and Timothy and tagged you in it and told all my followers you're amazing and I'm going to catch up with you and Timothy soon so now you *have* to introduce me to him, okay?"

She's what?

"You *what*?"

She laughs. "You're welcome."

And with that, she ends the call.

I blink. I *argh*. I throw up my hands and *argh* again.

And then I flinch as the car behind me blasts their horn, and I slam my foot on the accelerator.

Oh boy, what a weird start to the day.

3

T *im*

"Okay, so that went..." Lyle stops. Narrows his eyes. Considers his next word.

"Brilliantly?" I offer.

He lifts an eyebrow.

I laugh out a sigh and turn back to the streets blurring by outside the Audi.

The interview—live on the country's leading breakfast program, where I'd been scheduled to announce my move into federal politics, specifically for the seat of Grayndler in the upcoming House of Representatives by-election—had been a train wreck.

A spectacular one.

I'd been...preoccupied.

Preoccupied. Not exactly the right word.

Infatuated?

I hadn't been able to stop thinking about the woman who'd knocked me off my feet. Throughout the whole damn interview with the amiable and well-prepared breakfast show hosts, I kept wondering how I was going to go about running into her again.

How would I find her again?

Could I? Should I?

Would it be ethically wrong to make use of Dad's contacts?

Consequently, I'd got distracted during the interview and gone off on a rant about how the current federal government in charge was fucking over the country *and* the planet with their dogged obsession with coal.

I have a sinking feeling I might have actually even used the term *fucking over*.

Shit.

Thank God, we'd dropped Ellie off at school before the interview.

She didn't need to see her father involved in a train wreck. A train wreck where I'd utterly failed to mention I was imminently joining the ranks of federal politics in the very party I'd roasted for fucking over the country and planet, via the upcoming by-election for the seat of Grayndler.

The whole point of the interview.

I have a vague recollection of the hosts trying to steer the interview back to the scripted matter at hand.

I have an even vaguer recollection of staring off into the distance for a few seconds, trying to remember if the woman who'd knocked me off my feet had blue eyes or green. Or grey.

Or hazel.

Yeah. Train wreck.

"*Brilliantly* is not the word I'd use," Lyle deadpans. His phone vibrates in his hand with an incoming message and he glances at its screen.

I clear my throat. "Salvageable, though, yes?"

I have to get my act together. If nothing else, I'm presenting a report on the impact gas-seam mining is having on the pastoral lands in rural Australia to a consortium this afternoon. That report has the power to make or break—

Lyle leans forward in his seat and taps Colin's shoulder. "Fairwater House, Colin."

I stiffen. "What? No, that's not right. I've got a meeting with the Sydney Uni Environmental Sciences head. I need to—"

"Your father wants to see you."

"To *see* me?"

Lyle has the decency to look uncomfortable. A smidgin.

"For fuck's sake." I throw up my hands. "I'm not a naughty kid who needs an ear-bashing from his dad. I've got work to do." Leaning forward, I catch Colin's attention in the rearview mirror. "Sydney Uni, Colin. Please. Thanks."

"Colin," Lyle says, stare locked on the back of Colin's head. "Fairwater House."

"Colin," I echo—determined to keep my cool, no matter how infantile the situation. "Sydney Uni."

Colin coughs.

The Audi doesn't change course. It does, however, slow down somewhat.

"Colin," Lyle snaps.

Colin clears his throat and the SUV speeds up.

"Jesus." I slump in my seat. "I'm being abducted."

Colin clears his throat again. "Sorry, sir."

"Colin," I meet the older gentleman's eyes in the mirror once more, "you've known me almost my entire life. I'm pretty certain you even changed my nappy once or twice when I was a baby, right?"

"Seriously, Timothy?" Lyle wrinkles his nose. "Do you need to resort to toilet humour?"

"Do you need to resort to kidnapping?"

Colin chuckles. And then does a bad job of hiding the laugh in a cough.

Lyle glares at the back of his head. Again.

Silence stretches. I'm not in any hurry to break it. Screw it. I'm not the one doing the abducting. I stare out my window, trying not to grind my teeth. Great. Bloody great. One dodgy TV appearance and it's *Off to see Dad* time.

"I think," Lyle taps at his iPad's screen, "we can save this. Regroup, with the right plan. A few photos of you and Ellie with the new puppy released at the right time—this evening just when our target demographic tends to check their social media accounts. Yes, the new owner—you, happy but tired from having a new addition in the home. Yes, that could work quite well. We could spin this perfectly. Tired single-dad dog owner has moment of exhaustion on TV, but oh look how adorable he is with his puppy. Look how loving he is." Excitement fills his voice. "Of *course*, I want to vote for him. Absolutely I'd vote for him. He loves *dogs*!"

I gape at him. When was the last time I legitimately gaped? "Are you for real?"

"What do you think of this one?" He shows me the screen. Onscreen is a small white fluffy ball that is probably a dog.

I look at it. Look up at him. My eyebrows rise.

From behind the wheel, Colin clears his throat again.

"Or this?" Lyle swipes his finger over the screen, replacing the white ball of fluff with a slightly smaller white ball of fluff. This one is wearing a pastel-pink bow around its neck.

Colin once again clears his throat. Louder.

I look from the iPad to the driver, to outside the car.

Huh. We're currently not moving.

I look toward the front, out the windscreen.

Ah, we're stopped at a red light.

Which changes to green as I watch.

Colin coughs.

I meet his eyes in the mirror again.

Colin raises his eyebrows and flicks a quick glance to the left.

Behind us, someone beeps their car horn. Twice.

I look out my window. At the world beyond the Audi.

And open the door and climb out. "Tell Dad I said hi," I say, closing the door on the most shocked expression I've ever seen on Lyle's face.

The Audi pulls away, crossing the busy intersection with the flow of traffic.

I stand on the footpath, a grin splitting my face as Lyle's shocked expression gapes out at me through the Audi's back window as the traffic swallows it up.

"Thanks, Colin," I chuckle.

Dad's going to be unimpressed with the situation, but to be honest, I've made it a lifelong habit of not impressing the venerable Robert Holt with the decisions I've made. Playing field hockey instead of rugby in high school was just the start. Going on to become an environmentalist instead of a barrister when I finished my law degree was a nice follow-up.

The decision to follow him into politics will go a step toward bridging the divide between us.

I hope.

I chuckle again, wipe my hands together in an admittedly cliched that's-enough-of-that motion, and pivot on my heel.

I'll get a rideshare back home, change out of my clothes—I'm going to think of the woman who sent me flying every time I smell pineapple from now on. Not complaining—and then get my arse to the uni so I can—

My phone vibrates in my back pocket with an incoming text message.

I know it's not Dad or Lyle; both would call. Dad despises texting and in all the time I've known Lyle—three months of him planning my political arrival—he's never texted. Not once.

Feeling somewhat safe from a possible berating, I pull my phone free and read the message.

Frown at the message.

It's from Dan, my old brother-in-law.

So you're getting a dog? Els is going to be very excited.

A finger of anger drags up my spine. What the hell has Lyle done? I explicitly said no—

My phone vibrates again. This time the message is from Ellie's best friend's father, Amit.

Hi Tim. If you're happy with Chelsea Parker let me know. We're getting Mikki a puppy for her birthday. Don't mention it to Ellie yet though. Want it to be a surprise for Mikki.

I frown again. What the hell? Who's Chelsea Parker? What on earth is Amit on about?

I'm about to text him back when another text message flashes up on my phone's screen, this one from the female co-host of the breakfast show on which I crashed and burned barely an hour ago.

Hi Timothy. You should have mentioned your dog. Our viewers eat dog-stories up. Give me a call and we can maybe tee up another interview. Maybe you can bring your dog in for the segment. Samantha.

She follows this up with a dog emoji.

What. The. Fuck?

Something is going on. Something...weird. Something involving a dog. And someone called Chelsea Parker.

None of it makes sense, least of all the sudden onslaught of messages. It's as if something has just been broadcast or released or posted or...

"Ah, no," I mutter. Chest tight, standing right there on the

footpath, pedestrians hurrying pass me, I do the thing I swore
I'd never ever do.

Google myself.

My gut sinks as I look at my phone. Whoa, there's a lot of
stuff out there on the internet dedicated to me. Stuff I'm not
even going to look at. But nothing I can see seems to involve a
dog, not even in the current new posts.

I bite back a growl. Damn it, I'm going to have to do it. I'm
going to have to look at social media.

Shit.

I open Instagram. Lyle talks about appealing to the
Insta crowd often, as if they're a whole different race of
Australians, so I figure it's the best one to start with. I
type #TimothyHolt into the search field, click on
Recent and...

Oh. I see.

There I am, on my butt on the footpath out the front of my
apartment complex, smiling up at the woman who collided
with me. I tap the image to see if there's any info. Nope. All that
accompanies the image—posted by an account called
TimHoltAlways; Jesus, really?—is the caption: *Knocked off his
feet!!* Along with *#TimothyHolt* *#TimHoltAlways* and
#TimHoltIsHot

Tim Holt is hot? Jesus.

I scroll through to the second most recent post. This one is
the same image just slightly cropped closer with *#TimothyHolt-
theHottie* as the only caption. The next image I'm at least on my
feet, smiling wide at the woman.

Smiling quite a bit at her.

And she's smiling back.

Also quite a bit.

In fact, if I didn't know better, I'd say, based on the photo
alone, we were old friends.

No, *more* than old friends. With the way my body is reacting at the image now, *definitely* more than old friends.

I read the caption with this post.

Timothy Holt and mystery woman find happiness. Who is she? #TimothyHolt #eyefucking

I blink at that last hashtag. Eye fucking?

I look back at the photo of us. Yep, *eye fucking* is exactly what it looks like we're doing.

Tight heat curls through parts of me that haven't felt hot for a while. I knew I'd been...attracted to the woman from the footpath but with the way I'm looking at her in this photo...

Heart starting to thump, I scroll to the next most recent #TimothyHolt post.

It's the same at the previous, me and her, smiling at each other, no, *eye fucking* each other. But this post almost has a novel for a caption. It's posted by an account called Marjory_With_A_Why. Marjory_With_A_Why—whoever they are— has almost two million followers and is quite excited about my interaction with...

"Ahh. Chelsea Parker."

I look at my mystery woman; those parts of my body that are a bit hot get hotter.

According to the font of all knowledge that is Marjory, her name is Chelsea Parker, and she runs a dog training business called Oh Behave Dog Training and has, apparently, helped Marjory's dog Brutus. Marjory_With_A_Why informs everyone in her post Chelsea is amazing and brilliant and wonderful and an absolute treasure and anyone who needs some dog training should call her at Oh Behave Dog Training and OMG can you all believe my friend is friends *wink wink* with Timothy Holt? #TimothyHolt #LuckyGirl

There's a ridiculous list of hashtags after those but I don't read them. Instead, I look at Chelsea Parker again.

Chelsea Parker, dog trainer.

My throat thickens.

Would it be weird to track her down, now I know who she is, and ask her out? Would it be weird to call up her business and maybe arrange to see her again?

Would it?

Not if you own a dog, it wouldn't.

The thought whispers through my mind. Hooks into it.

I think of Lyle's scheme to seduce voters. I think of Ellie's pure joy and excitement at the slightest possibility of us getting a dog. I think of the way I'd felt when Chelsea had smiled at me back on the footpath outside my apartment complex...

I close Instagram and open Google.

My thumb hovers over the search field for a second. My heart pounds like a cannon in my chest.

Am I going to do what I think I'm going to do?

Am I?

Am I?

I pull in a deep breath and start typing with my thumb.

It seems I am.

God, help me.

4

Chelsea

MARJORY IS a freaking force of nature. That's only a partial compliment. You know when you were a kid flying a kite and you wanted the wind to blow hard and when it did it was fun for a few fleeting seconds until the wind turned to a Cat. 5 level gust and tried to rip it out of your hands and your shoulders out of their sockets, and you're whimpering and wondering where you went wrong with your life choices to bring you to this moment when you know you can't fight against it anymore and it's so hard?

My hour session with Marjory was like that.

I arrived. Brutus met me at the front door to her multi-million waterfront home, his manners perfect. His sit perfect.

Marjory beamed at me, proud of her dog. And then said, "So...Timothy Holt?"

"Honestly, Marjory," I'd replied, keeping my attention on

Brutus, who was doing a very good job of 'Eyes to me', "I don't know him."

"Oh." Marjory had smiled. "Okay."

The kite floating gently on the wind.

Forty minutes later, the onslaught of gale-force questions, suggestions, and bribery began.

By the time our session was over, I was as on-edge and frazzled as Brutus used to be before Marjory became a client—and that's a lot. Medication-level a lot.

I finally only managed to get out after I promised her I would 100% give him her number if I ever *did* run into him again and that I would 100% tell him she would love to 'do something for the environment' with him.

Brutus—a very good boy—covered me in dog kisses before I left. Although to be fair, I think he was just trying to sample as much of the dry pineapple juice on my shirt and jeans.

"Okay," I mutter, throwing myself into my car. "Okay."

Maybe having celebrity clients isn't as awesome as people think?

Craziness aside, I'm done for the morning. My next client isn't until 3pm which means I can go home and decompress with Gary.

I dig my phone out of my bag and go to turn it back on. And stop.

I look at the dark screen. At the complete and utter disconnection from the world.

I think I'll just keep it that way for a while.

Gary is sitting in his usual spot on the sofa in front of the living room window when I get home.

Home is a cozy split-level terrace in Glebe. It used to belong to my mum—a vet—when she was alive. I lived here with her in wonderful contentment until she passed away from a stroke three years ago. My father...well, I didn't know anything about him except he was a violent drunk my mum had a one-night stand with thirty-eight years ago. The only thing I got from him was a half brother, Angus, whom I adore.

Of course, I didn't know Angus existed until my dad wrapped himself around a tree in a car accident when I was fifteen.

Angus is one of Australia's best chefs and the only family I have.

Him and Gary.

Gary, as usual, gets himself all worked up at my arrival. For an old dog, he still knows how to put on a welcome-home-hooman show. His tail knocks the TV remote control off the coffee table as he barks his version of hello.

"I missed you too," I say, giving both of his ears a gentle scruff. "Wanna go to the park?"

Of course, the answer is yes. The answer is always yes.

We go to the park. I don't take my phone.

This walk, the park walk, is Gary's favourite. It's a slow amble where Gary gets to dictate the speed as his nose explores everything, what I call a 'snuffle walk'. Snuffle walks are vital to a dog's well-being and enrichment. I tell clients to give their dogs at least one snuffle walk a day.

We amble home almost an hour later, Gary carrying the stick he'd found with pure doggo delight.

Approaching my front gate, I'm turning my phone back on —better get back into work mode for the afternoon—when I realise someone is standing on my tiny front porch.

Watching me.

TIM

. . .

THREE LEGS.

Only three.

Two at the back, one at the front.

I stand at the enclosure's door, looking through its cold metal bars at the hip-high wiry-coated mutt looking back at me from the far corner.

I'd come directly to the animal shelter after my escape from the Audi, thanks to a Google search and an Uber driver who hardly said a word. I should have gone to work. I had a meeting after all.

I should have come here after that.

But the pull in my gut to come now...well, sometimes I let my gut make decisions my brain wouldn't.

I'd walked into the shelter, asked to see the dogs. And now, here I am. Looking at a three-legged dog who's looking back at me, clearly scared.

Its ears are drooped, and its tail is so tucked, I can't tell if it actually has one. It watches me, amber eyes reflecting the harsh overhead fluorescent lights.

Three legs.

Why does it have only three legs?

I slide my attention to the hand-written info card taped to the bars next to the door.

Wilbur. Mixed breed. 4 yrs old. Surrendered.

Nothing about the AWOL front left leg. Nothing about why the dog was surrendered.

A heavy weight presses on my chest and I look back at the dog. At Wilbur.

He's still watching me. Ears still drooped. Tail still tucked.

A strange sensation stirs somewhere deep inside me, and I shift away from the bars a little.

Wilbur's ears prick. They're big and floppy and make me feel that strange sensation even more.

"Wilbur," I say, softly.

A tail appears. Not quite tucked anymore but still not fully on display. A shy little swipe from side to side. The heavy weight on my chest grows heavier at the sight of it: it has an unnatural blunt end. At some point in Wilbur's life, his tail has been cut short.

Why? Who did it? Was it done under aesthetic?

"Hey, Wilbur," I say, keeping my voice calm and gentle.

His ears prick again and his tail lashes side to side faster, his whole body wobbling side to side with it. He stumbles a little—the lack of a front left leg clearly impacts his balance somewhat—but his tail doesn't stop wagging.

Chest heavy, that strange sensation swelling through me, I slowly crouch down and extend my hand through the bars.

Wilbur's tail slows down, and he watches me. Wary. That's the word that comes to mind. Wary.

My heart breaks.

"Hey, Wilbur," I say again. "It's okay, boy."

His ears prick again. His tail speeds up.

"It's okay," I repeat, smiling. "It's—"

My fucking phone rings, Darth Vader's theme—the ringtone I've set for Lyle—blaring throughout the pound.

Dogs start barking. And barking. And barking.

Wilbur cowers away from the sound, tail disappearing, ears drooping.

Fuck.

Staying in my crouch, keeping my hand extended through the bars, palm down, fingers loose, I yank my phone from my pocket and ram it to my ear. "What?"

"Where are...wait." Confusion fills Lyle's voice. "Is that...is that *barking*? What are you—"

"I gotta go," I say. Wilbur's ears are pricking again. And the slight hint of a tail wag makes my heart skip a beat.

"Timothy," Lyle almost shouts. "You can't just get any old dog. There's focus groups to consider and—"

I kill the connection, flick my phone to mute with my thumbnail, and shove it back into my pocket. "There we go," I say to Wilbur. "Better?"

His tail wags more.

I smile. "He's annoying, but his heart's in the right place."

He takes a couple of steps towards me again.

I keep my hand—the one still in his enclosure—motionless, my fingers relaxed.

Slowly, very slowly, he approaches it.

My heart clenches. I hold my breath.

He pauses, his amber eyes looking into mine for a split second, and then his nose touches the backs of my fingers.

My breath escapes me on a shaky sigh.

I let him sniff my hand. I want to pat him, I want to stroke my fingers over his head and let him know everything is going to be okay, that everything horrible that happened to him in his life is in the past, that nothing horrible is going to happen to him again. But I stay still. I've never had a dog—Dad wasn't a fan and Mum pretty much followed along with whatever Dad decreed—but I've seen *How to Train Your Dragon* a gazillion times. It's Ellie's favourite movie. I know the last thing you do when interacting with a skittish animal is rush them. You let them dictate the pace. You let them learn they can trust you. That you're not a threat. That you're not going to hurt them.

I stay in a crouch, my knees killing me, my phone silently vibrating away in my pocket—Lyle, most likely—and let Wilbur explore my hand as thoroughly as he wants with his nose.

"It's okay, mate," I murmur, as he gives me a quick look again. "It's okay."

His tails wags. A lot. And he rubs his head under my fingers and against my palm.

And I'm in love.

Something hot and prickly stings the back of my eyes. "It's okay, mate," I repeat, and yep, my voice is croaky. I pat him as much as I can through the bars. His tail is wagging so much he's wobbling side to side again. It's beautiful. Poetry in motion. "Everything is going to be okay."

I stand. Wilbur's ears droop. How many times since he's been in here has he watched someone walk away from him?

"I'll be back," I promise him.

His tail wags. A little.

No fucking way am I going to not be back. If I had bolt cutters, I'd have him out now.

The woman behind the counter raises her eyebrows when I tell her I want to adopt Wilbur.

"Are you sure?"

A little finger of anger shoots through me. "I'm sure."

"He's a beautiful dog," she says. "With the sweetest nature, but he comes with some baggage."

Baggage? Ha. Try growing up with the leader of the country as your father.

"How did he lose his leg?" I ask.

She shakes her head, her expression growing sad. "We don't know. We found him chained to the shelter's front gate over twelve weeks ago. No chip, no collar, very malnourished, and terrified. One of the volunteers christened him Wilbur after a teddy bear they had as a kid that was missing a leg."

With every word, my anger grows. Towards the person who'd abandoned Wilbur, and the world for letting people like that get away with doing so.

"I'm ready to take him now," I state. "Now now."

She frowns. "Now now? As in, *now*?"

Of course, I have no actual way of getting Wilbur home, mind you. I'm a fair way from Balmain right now. Do rideshares allow people to have pets? Doesn't matter. Whatever I need to do, I'll do. Maybe I could call Colin? And swear him to secrecy about Wilbur.

Lyle is going to have a seizure.

Ellie is going to go crazy. I picture her excitement. Feel it in my heart already.

I also picture Lyle's exasperation. Wilbur isn't the photo-op/breakfast TV show dog Lyle has in mind. I'm failing very badly at this political career already, it seems. And I haven't even started it yet.

And then I picture Chelsea Parker, dog-trainer extraordinaire. I picture her smiling at me. I picture her smiling at Ellie. I picture her patting Wilbur...

I'm not prepared for the heavy weight that wraps around my chest. That picture? Me, Ellie, Chelsea, and Wilbur?

Yeah, that picture knocks me sideways.

"I applaud your enthusiasm, sir," the woman behind the counter says, "but there're steps. Procedures. We have to make sure your home is suitable to start with."

Pulling out my phone, I do something I swore I would never do. Ever. Opening Google, I enter my name into the search field, wait for my image to fill it, and then present her the screen. "See this? I'm him. That's me. Timothy Holt. Prime Minister Robert Holt's son."

She gapes at the phone. At me. At the phone again. "Oh wow," she whispers. "The first time I ever voted in an election I voted for your father," she continues, just as soft, just as starstruck. "He was a *good* prime minister."

And I've got her. Just like that.

A tiny tickle of guilt feathers up my spine, but I ignore it.

I'm not deserting Wilbur. I'm not leaving him here for a minute longer.

I shove my phone back into my pocket, place my hands on the counter, lean a little closer to the woman behind it, and give her my best I'm-your-future-Prime-Minister-smile. "He was. And he'd love Wilbur." I smile wider. "Now, let's go get the key and unlock the cage, because I'm walking out of here with him today."

5

C *helsea*

"YOU'RE ALL OVER SOCIAL MEDIA," Angus says, removing his sunglasses to cast me a bemused look from my front porch.

Tail wagging, Gary barks an excited hello. He loves Angus. Maybe as much as I do.

My stomach tightens, even as an image of Timothy Holt and his smile flashes through my head. "Why?"

Either Marjory's destroying my business and career because I haven't produced him already, or—

"Apparently you're in a scorching sexual relationship with our ex-PM's son." Angus cocks an eyebrow as he gives Gary a scratch behind the ears. "I don't know whether to be an over-protective brother and grumble about it, or a little hurt you haven't mentioned it to me yet."

"Well, you know me," I say, my girlie parts joining my

stomach in getting all tight at the thought of being in a sexual relationship with Timothy Holt. "I don't kiss and tell."

Angus narrows his eyes.

I snort, shoving my phone into my jeans' back pocket. There are way too many messages and missed calls for my state of mind right now. "Seriously. I literally bumped into him on the footpath at Balmain. Had no clue who he was. The only thing I knew was he was cute."

"Cute?"

"Insanely cute," I clarify. "I spilt my pineapple juice all over him."

"Very impressive move, there, sis. If you're going to tell me you licked it off, I'm outta here."

"Angus!" I roll my eyes. "Gross."

He grins. And then gives me a stern scowl. "Well, it's all over social media you're banging each other six ways to Sunday."

"Social media? Since when do you do social media? I thought you were still trying to hide away from the public eye after that magazine article?"

Angus was recently named Australia's Bachelor of the Year —much to his conflicted embarrassment.

"I *don't* do social media. But when my entire lunch staff is gossiping about what my sister is doing and who she's doing it with, I pay attention. And get my arse over to said sister to give her an over-protective big brother chat."

"*Argh!*" I throw up my hands.

Gary barks.

Angus laughs.

"Marjory is holding the whole thing over my head," I complain, unlocking my front door. To be honest, I'm surprised Angus didn't let himself in. He has a key. "If I don't introduce her to my new famous *boyfriend*"—I make the air quote signs with my fingers—"she'll destroy my business."

Striding into my place, Angus chuckles.

"It's not funny," I protest, following.

Gary scampers in, indiscriminately drops his slobber-coated ball and proceeds to drink an entire ocean's worth from his water bowl in the kitchen.

"I'm sorry," Angus says over his shoulder. "You're right. It's not. I'd be worried if an influential Instagrammer threatened the restaurant's reputation." He snatches up my laptop from the coffee table, opens it, and drops into one of my armchairs. "Let's see what we can do."

I plonk down beside him, loving that he wants to help. I have no clue how he can, but the fact he wants to... I'd give him a hug, but he's not big on hugs. Thanks to our father's...not so wonderful parenting skills, Angus isn't one for physical contact. "Any chance you could bake up a magical gingerbread Timothy Holt?"

He laughs, navigating to Google. He types *Tim Holt* into the search field, hits Send and sits back. The screen fills with images of the man I collided with on the footpath in Balmain and my girlie parts do their tightening thing again. "Damn, he's cute," I mutter.

"Not really my type," Angus mutters back, with a sideways smirk at me.

I laugh, even as I check out all the images of Timothy Holt on the screen.

He *is* cute. Too cute. Even if Marjory is correct and he is looking at me like I'm a warm fresh croissant and he wants to eat me up—Marjory's words, not mine—he's in a whole different league.

Look, I know I'm not *un*attractive, but I'm not ex-PM's-son level okay?

I've got amazing hair. My features seem to tick most people's boxes and a lifetime of walking/running with dogs means I'm fairly fit. True, I probably eat way too much chocolate, but I look okay.

However, I didn't go to an expensive private school, I'm pretty certain any Grammar Nazi would crucify me based on most of my emails, and I'm dressed by Target most of the time. Plus, there's the fact I didn't vote for his dad. Or his dad's party. As far as political things go, I fall considerably *left* of what Robert Holt and his party stand for.

"Okay, plan."

Angus's voice drags me back to the living room. "Plan?"

Angus nods. "Plan. I'll invite him to the restaurant for an 'exclusive' dinner tomorrow night and you'll just so happen to be sitting at the table next to his. Easy."

I think of the way Timothy Holt smiled at me. The way I felt when he did. The way I'd smiled back...

"What if he's busy tomorrow night?" I ask. God, am I really considering this?

Angus looks at me like I've sprouted an extra head. "No one turns down a personal invitation from me to eat at *Buckley's Chance*, Chelsea."

I give him a dubious look.

"Seriously," he says. "Do you have any clue how many months the restaurant is already fully booked? Getting a reservation, especially for dinner on a Saturday night, is almost impossible."

My eyebrows shoot up.

"Remember when the Canadian Prime Minister ate at *Buckley's Chance* during his last visit to Australia? I invited him. He said yes."

"Okay, okay." I laugh again. "I believe you."

Who knew one of the perks of being an award-winning

chef was influential power? At least it hasn't gone to Angus's head. Not that I can see, at least.

A thought occurs to me, and I frown. "But wait, if it's impossible to get a table at your restaurant for months and months, how are you suddenly going to have *two* available tomorrow night?"

He chuckles. "Sis, just trust me, okay?"

"Okay." I always have. From the moment I first met him, when he was sixteen and I was fifteen the day before our father's funeral. From that moment on, I never doubted Angus would be there for me if I ever needed him.

He lifts an eyebrow. "So, you're good with the plan?"

My stomach does its little knotty twist again and I let out a shaky sigh. "I'm good with the plan. But remember, it's to save my business and not because I want to get into Timothy Holt's pants?"

Angus scowls, shaking his head as he deposits my laptop back on the coffee table. "I do *not* want to know anything about his pants and your location in regards to them."

"Where's your sense of adventure?" I tease, even as my sex fills with a tight heat. Stupid sex. Getting all excited over a plan that really has no hope of succeeding.

"In the kitchen, where it belongs." He digs his phone out of his back pocket. "I'll call Kara and get her to—"

Gary bursts into wild barking, a second before someone rings my doorbell.

"Hey, hey, hey," I soothe, scrambling to my feet to give him a calming pat. "It's okay. It's just someone at the door."

He barks again, his cheery oh-if-that's-all-it-is bark, and goes back to his spot on the sofa.

Whoever is at the door rings the bell again.

Angus throws a faint frown at the front door as he lifts the phone to his ear. "Clearly, they're impa—Kara, I need VIP tables times two set up for tomorrow night." He sighs, lips curling. "Sorry, sorry. Hi, Kara. Hello. How are you?"

I chuckle, heading for the door.

"I'm at Chelsea's place," I hear him tell his sous chef. "What do you mean, why am I there? I left when you started to lose your shit over that Instagram— What do you *mean*, you didn't even notice I was gone?"

I laugh again. The pair of them fight and insult each other regularly. Angus tells me it's a chef/sous chef thing. I think it's a weird thing, but there's no denying it works for them. The food at *Buckley's Chance* is incredible.

The doorbell rings a third time.

Gary lets out a bark, tail wagging.

"All right, all right," I mutter, quickening my pace.

"It's Timothy Holt," Angus calls from the armchair, devilish jest in his voice. "Come to—what? Oh, for God's sake, Kara, get back to work. Kara says hi."

"Hi, Kara," I call back, almost at the door.

"I've hung up already," Angus informs me. "So tomorrow night—"

The doorbell rings a *fourth* time.

"Are you serious?" I shake my head. "Who the hell is this impatient?"

"It's definitely Tim," Angus declares, even more devilish jest in his voice. "Come to give you the bill for spilling pineapple juice all over his shirt. Good thing your big brother is here to make sure he doesn't take advantage of—"

"Oh my *God*," I groan, throwing him a look over my shoulder. "Stop."

He grins, shoving his phone back into his pocket.

I turn to the door—fighting the ridiculous, deluded hope trying to build in me that it *might*, in fact, be Timothy Holt on the other side of the threshold—and open it.

The man from the footpath is on the other side. Not Timothy Holt but the *other* man. The slicked-back millennial. The one who kept glaring at me.

Lyle.

True to form, he fixes a level glare at me. "Chelsea Parker? I'm Lyle Asher, Timothy Holt's publicist. I need to have a chat with you, if I may?"

I blink.

He smiles. It doesn't reach his eyes. "Now."

My eyebrows shoot up. I can feel my forehead wrinkle. "Excuse me?"

I hear footsteps behind me. And the soft clack-clack of Gary's claws on the floorboards. His warm, furry body presses against the side of my knee just as Angus stops beside me, one elbow on the doorframe, the other slung around my shoulder.

"Hi," Angus says, eyeing Lyle off like the protective big brother he is. "Some manners would be nice."

Lyle turns a narrow-eyed gaze at Angus, studies him for a second, and then is suddenly all sunshine and beaming smiles. "Ah. Sorry. I misunderstood an earlier situation when Chelsea and I first met and I wanted to have a conversation with her about it, but I see I don't need to."

I blink. Again. What the?

Angus straightens from the doorframe, his arm curling around my shoulder more. He's tall. Taller than Lyle. For a chef, he's an intimidating sod when he wants to be. "That so." He gives me a sideways look. "You okay with this guy just turning up here, Chels?"

A part of me wants to laugh. God love Angus. Another part of me is pissed. It's clear Lyle Asher came here to scare me off for some reason, but now assumes Angus is my partner—bleh. Gross—and has decided I'm no...what? threat to Timothy Holt's...something? Reputation? Social status? Career? What the hell did he think I was going to do? Stalk his boss? Throw myself at him?

Well, you are *letting Angus use his restaurant's popularity to "bump into" him again.*

I twist my lips, glaring at Lyle. Come to think of it, how the hell did he get my address? Who the hell does he think he is?

The political advisor to the ex-Prime Minister's son.

I suppress a shaky sigh.

Good grief, I'm beginning to regret taking Marjory on as a client. No publicity is worth this kind of surreal stress.

"I'm okay with this guy just leaving," I say to Angus, giving Lyle a level look. "But not before I point out my home address isn't public knowledge."

Lyle has the decency to look a smidgen contrite before he smiles at Angus again. "I was merely worried Chelsea might be thinking of pursuing a situation not in...anyone's best interest. But obviously, I was worrying needlessly."

Anyone's? Translation: Timothy's.

Angus doesn't say anything. Just holds Lyle's stare. His expression very clearly says *I don't like you. Go away.*

Lyle looks at me. Does a jerky little nod. "Okay, now that's cleared up." He pivots and hurries away from my front door. I spy a low red sports car—a Porsche, I think—parked in my driveway. He gets into it without a backward look at me and turns over the engine.

Why am I not surprised Lyle would drive a Porsche?

"What the fuck was that?" Angus asks, as I close the door.

Gary, back on the sofa again, barks, as if to reiterate the question.

I bite my bottom lip. "I think he thought you were my... y'know."

Angus snorts. "Okay. Gross. But okay. So he came to warn you to what? Stay away from Timothy Holt?"

"I think so?"

A gleam flickers in Angus's eyes. A twitch plays with his lips. "In that case..." He pulls his phone from his pocket, jabs his thumb over its screen a few times and then presses it to his ear. "Kara, change of plans. I need you to cancel every reservation for tomorrow night."

I gasp. So does Kara. The sound damn near bursts from the phone. "What are you—"

Angus holds up his finger, a look of smug determination on his face. "Yeah, yeah, whatever. Give everyone a voucher. A free three-course meal or something. I need the restaurant empty of diners tomorrow night. I'm doing a private function for two. Who do you think?"

"No!" I shake my head furiously. "No, I'm not going to let you do that."

He frowns. "Okay, okay. Kara, *don't* cancel everyone's reservations, But do make sure the best two tables in the house are reserved. Number Six and Number Seven. Set them up close to each other. Oh, and I need Timothy Holt's phone number, his personal phone number, not the one for his P—" He laughs. "Of *course*, you already have it. I've told you you're amazing, right? No? Okay, well, you're amazing."

He ends the call, grin wide. He's very happy with himself.

"You're insane," I say, as he taps his thumb some more on his phone's screen. "I don't know what you think you're—"

"Hey," he says, giving me a look that makes me love him a million times more as he raises his phone to his ear. "I don't care who you work for. You don't come to my sister's house and try to make her feel inferior. Fuck that for a joke."

Gary barks in agreement.

Fuck that for a joke indeed.

6

T *im*

TURNS OUT, Wilbur loves being in a car.

Sitting on my lap in the backseat of the only dog-friendly Uber I could book, he sticks his head as far out the window as I'll let him, ears flapping in the breeze, tongue lolling out of his smiling mouth.

And it's definitely smiling. I have a happy, three-legged dog on my lap. Every now and again he pulls his head back into the car, licks my face, and then goes back to feeling the rush outside the window.

My credit card took an absolute beating at the shelter, but it's worth it. I walked out of that place with Wilbur, a brand-new collar for him, a harness for walking, a lead, a food bowl, and a bag of black flat shapes the shelter worker—Tess—called liver treats.

"Pretty much all dogs love liver treats," she'd said as she bagged everything up. "They're fantastic for training."

The moment she'd said the word *training*, an image of Chelsea Parker had filled my head.

And it's been there ever since.

Who am I kidding? The image of Chelsea Parker has taken up residence in my head—rent free—since she bumped into me back in Balmain.

Added to the sheer joy that is Wilbur, and this day is a whole shift in everything I thought I wanted and needed.

A part of me wants to ask my driver, Anton, if he'll swing by Ellie's school so I can surprise her with the new edition to our family.

And then I remember I'm meant to be in a meeting and decide to take Wilbur with me to that instead. And when I collect Ellie from school, he can be sitting up in the backseat, ready to meet her.

Basically, whenever possible, where I go, Wilbur will go. That's one of my new life philosophies.

Without any provocation, Chelsea Parker fills my head again. I wonder what she'll make of Wilbur? Of course, she'll love him from the get-go. Who wouldn't?

So call her. Now. You've never owned a dog in your life. You need help to train him. Call her. You have a legit reason. This is the legit reason. Call her. Arrange to see her. Take Wilbur. And Ellie. Maybe Thornton Park? Or Peacock Point Reserve? Maybe take a picnic lunch? Ask her to stay? Ask her if she wants to go for dinner after? Maybe—

Wilbur enthusiastically licks my face again, body vibrating as he wags his stumpy tail.

"What do you think about meeting Chelsea Parker at Thornton Park, mate?" I ask, giving him a scratch around his ears.

He's impressed with the idea. If his happy woof is anything to go by.

"He's a cool dog," Anton says from behind the wheel.

"He's a very cool dog," I agree.

"You're our ex-PM's son, right?"

"I am." Another out-of-character moment. I don't normally confirm who I am so quickly.

Anton nods. "Thought so. Saw you on the TV this morning."

"You did?"

He laughs. "Did you know you said *fuck* twice on live TV?"

Twice? Jesus. Maybe my political career is dead before it can even truly begin? I let out a wry laugh. "Fuck, eh?"

Lyle would kill me if he was here right now.

Anton laughs again. "Next time, take your dog on with you. No one would care about the swearing then."

"Good plan." Maybe I should employ Anton to be my PR guy.

Yeah, like Lyle—and Dad—would agree to that.

"Can I ask a question?" I give Wilbur, now sniffing the air just beyond the window, another scratch around the ears.

"Sure. Hit me."

"Do you trust politicians?"

His laughter comes from his belly and bounces around the interior of his Subaru Forester. "Fuck no."

"What about a politician with a three-legged dog?"

He snorts. Before he can answer, my phone vibrates into life in my pocket.

Guilt hits me. I've ignored it for too long. I have to face whatever music Lyle's prepared to blare at me. I pulled my phone free, frowning.

Unknown number. Hmm.

I connect the call even though I normally never answer an

unknown number—what the hell. Wilbur's put me in a good mood—and press it to my ear. Wilbur thinks this is lots of fun and tries to eat it out of my hand.

Chuckling, doing my best to move my phone/hand/head out of his mouth's range, I say, "Tim Holt speaking."

"Hi, Tim Holt," a male voice says on the other end. "This is Angus Daniels, the owner and head chef of *Buckley's Chance*. I'd like to personally invite you to an exclusive dinner at the restaurant tomorrow night."

Buckley's Chance?

Okay, if this is Lyle's doing, I'm impressed. I've never eaten at the five-star restaurant situated on Sydney Harbour with multi-million-dollar views of the Opera House. Trying to get a table there is damn near impossible. Maybe if I'd ever thought to play the Do-You-Know-Who-My-Father-Is card, a table would have become available, but until today, until making sure Wilbur left the shelter with me, I've never played that card at all.

If Lyle is trying to butter me up before insisting I do something I'd rather not for my future political coming out, I'll happily let him do so if it means eating at Buckley's Chance.

"What time?" I ask.

"Eight."

I don't know why, but I get the feeling Angus Daniels is grinning. He seems very happy with the conversation so far. The guy has cooked for and served some of the world's biggest celebrities and dignitaries, so I'm a small fish to him. And from what I've seen in the articles I've read about him in the various weekend newspaper supplements and Qantas inflight magazines, I never would have pegged him for a fan of Dad.

"I'll be there."

Chelsea Parker pops into my head. Again. Smiling at me.

"And I'm bringing a plus—"

Wilbur finally succeeds in his efforts to obtain my phone with his mouth.

By the time I've got it back from him—a little bit soggy with dog slobber—the call is disconnected. Possibly from Wilbur's teeth. Possibly because Angus has already done what he wanted to do.

Who knows with chefs? Especially famous ones like Daniels. Control freaks, the lot of them, from what I understand.

It doesn't matter. I now have *two* reasons to contact Chelsea Parker. One: to ask her to help me train Wilbur—first lesson: don't eat phones—and two: to invite her to dinner with me at Buckley's Chance to discuss *how* she's going to help me train Wilbur.

Is it subterfuge?

Maybe?

Am I doing it?

Yes. I mean, I *had* planned to contact her today after all, and say "Hi. Remember me? The guy you spilt pineapple juice on this morning? Would you like to help me train my dog?" And then I'd planned, maybe after chatting with her for a little while, or maybe after our first session with Wilbur, to ask her if she wanted to grab coffee with me one day? This was kind of the same thing, just a little bit more...grandiose, right? Maybe she would expect this kind of thing from the son of Robert Holt, ex-PM, anyways?

So now, I get to call her and say "Hi. Remember me? The guy you spilt pineapple juice on this morning? Would you like to help me train my dog? And have dinner with me at Buckley's Chance tomorrow night?"

I pat Wilbur. He wags his tail. Licks my face. Shoves his head out the window. The happiest dog I've ever seen.

"She's going to love you, mate," I tell him, my grin wide.

Yep. I'm doing this. I'm ready. The universe is giving me all the signs. I've got an awesome dog, and a table at an amazing restaurant normally impossible to get a table at. And, added bonus, Lyle is nowhere to be seen or heard.

I wipe my phone on my sleeve, give Wilbur a pat, and google Chelsea Parker's business name.

Smile at its name: Oh Behave Dog Training.

Hit call.

And press my phone to my ear again.

CHELSEA

"HMMM." Angus frowns at me. "We might..." He stops. Sucks his lips back into his mouth. "Umm..."

"What?" If it weren't for the fact I know what our father did to him, how brutal and violent he was to Angus and Angus's mum, I'd whack him with the back of my hand. "*What*?"

Angus rubs at the back of his neck. "We got cut off, but I think he started to say something about bringing a plus—"

My phone bursts into life.

I jump.

So does Angus.

Gary doesn't care. He's now dozing on the sofa.

Pulling my phone from my back pocket, I scowl at the unknown number, and connect the call. One of the downsides to running your own business? You can't really ignore unknown numbers. You don't answer, they go find another dog trainer.

"Oh Behave Dog Training," I say into the phone. "This is Chelsea."

"Hi, Chelsea," a male voice says. A familiar male voice.

Oh.

Boy.

My heart slams up into my throat like a pole vaulter on speed. My stare snaps to Angus. My stomach clenches. My girlie parts...

"This is Tim Holt," Timothy Holt, the target of Angus's machinations, says. "I don't know if you knew who I was this morning, but you bumped into me in the footpath at Balmain and—"

"I am so sorry," I burst out.

He laughs. "For?"

For? For?

I stare harder at Angus, who's looking at me like I've sprouted a second head.

For letting my brother try to set you up in a lame attempt to set us *up.*

"For spilling pineapple juice on you," I say.

Timothy—Tim—laughs again, and I picture his smile. God, his smile is yummy. "All good. Honest. I've got a seven-year-old. Trust me, pineapple juice is far from the most heinous thing to have spilt on me. Besides, it's me who should be apologising."

The image in my head of his smile is instantly replaced by the image of the federal police about to ram down my door. Oh crap. The cops are coming to arrest me because I physically assaulted the ex-PM's son. Accidentally, but still. And he's giving me a five second warning.

"Why?" I ask, heart palpitating. Am I too young for heart palpitations? Surely, I'm too young, right?

Angus is still staring at me. He makes a *Who is it?* face.

Tim lets out a chuckle that sounds...nervous? What the hell does he have to be nervous about? I'm the one about to get arrested. "I kind of used...err...social media to find out who you were."

My heart decides to return to the rhythm of a healthy—if somewhat excited and confused—thirty-seven-year-old.

Angus waves his hand around: *Tell me who it is!*

"Social media?" I say.

Another one of those nervous chuckles tumbles through the phone. "Umm... Do you know... I mean, you know I'm..." He sighs. "I'm Robert Holt's son. The ex-prime minister."

I gasp. A loud, melodramatic gasp.

Angus blanches. Gary lifts his head and looks at me, tail wagging.

"You already knew that," Tim says, and I can't help but smile at the deadpan mirth in his voice. "Didn't you."

"I did." I smile some more. Bite my lip. Angus gives me that *Who the hell is it?* face again.

Tim laughs. "My ego was feeling a little bruised there for a while."

"Oh, I *didn't* know who you were when I ran into you," I correct, grinning. I'm enjoying myself way too much.

"Ahh," Angus exclaims under his breath. "I see." He frowns. "I think." He shakes his head. "Maybe not. Why's he calling—"

Tim's laughter slips through the phone again. My girly parts react to the sound, and I turn my back to my brother. Is it possible to experience a mini orgasm just from hearing something? Probably not, but I'd rather not be looking at my brother when I'm feeling...frisky.

"Well, I'm Tim Holt," Tim says, and once more my head is full of images of him and his smile and his eyes and his shoulders and, oh boy, insta-lust here we come. "And I made full and possibly a little creepyish use of my...err...fame to discover who you were via the images of us together posted on social media this morning. So I could call you."

Us together.

So I could call you.

Us together.

I swallow, trying not to see too much into this surreal turn of events.

Us together. He said it. Us together.

"Why?" I ask a second time.

To ask you to dinner. How amazing would it be if he asks you to dinner?

"I have a three-legged dog," he says.

I blink.

Is that a euphemism for something?

"You what?"

"What?" Angus whispers, suddenly in front of me again.

"I have a dog," Tim states. There's an emotion in his voice I haven't heard before. It sends a delicious little ripple of something through me, and my nipples harden. I turn away from Angus again. "Wilbur. He's awesome. And I'm hoping you can help me train him."

Dog training.

I close my eyes. My shoulders slump, the delicious little ripple sliding away. "You'd like to engage my dog training services?"

What, in all honesty, was I expecting? An invitation to dinner? An invitation to fly away with him to Madrid or Paris or somewhere romantic and exotic? A marriage proposal?

I'm a dog trainer, and he's a revered environmentalist *and* the ex-PM's son.

"I would," he says. The nervous lilt is back. Why? Is he worried I'm not as good as the client testimonials on my website say? "Very much so. ASAP, if that's doable. Wilbur is, as I said, awesome, and I want to make sure I'm not responsible for him not being awesome. Does that make sense?"

It does. If I wasn't already halfway in love with this guy, the emotion in his voice when he talks about his dog, and the implication behind what he's said—*I know if my dog isn't having his best life, it's because of me*—slingshots me there immediately.

"It does," I actually manage to croak out.

Angus is once more in front of me. Confusion reigns supreme on his face. *What the hell is going on?* he mouths.

Tim clears his throat. "So, I'm hoping, *wondering* if we can have a meeting to discuss what you do. Tomorrow? At eight? I've got a table at Buckley's Chance. Do you know where that is?"

My mouth falls open. My heart is racing. Greyhound-level racing. I look at Angus.

What? he asks wordlessly. *What?*

"I *do* know where Buckley's Chance is," I say.

Here it comes, in five, four, three...

Angus's eyebrows shoot up. His mouth falls open. And then he laughs. Throws back his head and, stamping one foot on my floor, laughs. I snatch up a cushion from the sofa and shove it at him: *Shut up!* Gary bounds off the sofa, instantly and enthusiastically ready to join in the fun, and leaps up and around Angus with excited, happy yips.

"Are you..." Tim clears his throat again. "So yes? That's a yes? Eight okay? At Buckley's Chance? I can pick you up if you like? At your place?"

I stare at Angus.

Angus stares at me.

So does Gary.

What the hell do I say?

"Let's start with meeting Wilbur," I croak out.

Damn, being so professional. Sure, it's what I do with all my new or prospective clients: meet them and their dog or dogs at their place before establishing a training program, but still; I could have said yes to dinner with Tim Holt. Not a *date* dinner, but *still*, dinner!

"Okay. That makes sense." Is he happy with my answer? Tim Holt is most likely used to things going his way. "Today? I'm available in...bugger, Five hours. Is that okay?"

Can I go to Tim Holt's place in five hours?

Do I really need to think about that?

"Five hours is fine. Can you text me your address, please?" I'm trying to be calm and professional and business-like, when all I want to do is dance around the living room and punch the air and panic about what to wear, and oh my God, Marjory is going to be so impressed with me.

7

T *im*

WILBUR IS the star of my meeting.

The dean of the uni's environmental science department tries to steal him.

The CEO of the Environment Institute of Australia and New Zealand stops listening halfway through what I'm saying —it's imperative we need to convince the federal government to start funding renewables *now* before the country becomes an international pariah—and spends his time trying to teach Wilbur how to shake hands.

The chief executive from the CSIRO spends a substantial amount of time drafting up a prosthetic leg contraption he assures me he could get the engineering team to build.

At this point in time, I'm thinking Wilbur is bad for the environment.

But I know he's going to be good for Ellie.

We're sitting in the pick-up zone of her school, five cars back, waiting in line to collect her. Wilbur's head is out the window. His tail is wagging. His body is wobbling side to side.

After my meeting, Anton—dog-friendly rideshare driver and potential future political advisor—drove us home to my place.

"Worth more than five stars, my friend," I'd told him, as we pulled to a halt outside my apartment building.

His answering grin had been wide and pointed. "Then tip me well."

I had.

Wilbur had spent an unholy amount of time sniffing everything. On the sidewalk, in the foyer, the lift, the front door to my apartment, and every inch inside it.

We had a brief moment of chaos when he discovered Lord Byron and pranced along the hallway with Ellie's cherished teddy bear dangling from his mouth by one fuzzy arm. I made a lunge for Byron, Wilbur tucked tail and did a little pee on the floor, dropping the bear.

Slammed with guilt, I scooped up both Wilbur and Byron. "It's okay, mate," I told Wilbur. "It's okay."

He gave my face a lick.

I showed him Byron. "Off-limits."

Even in my arms, he tried to take Bryon in his mouth again. Hmmm, this could be a problem.

"Let's get Chelsea onto this one, hey?" I murmured to him, tossing Byron onto Ellie's bed and closing the door.

Out in the kitchen, I gave him a drink, a few of the liver treats, and then, after quite a few minutes doing nothing but chilling together, we climbed into my Volvo and headed for Ellie's school.

And now here we are. Fourth in line.

Wilbur's tail is wagging so much as he watches the never-ending flow of kids streaming out of the school and past us, he keeps losing his footing.

Doesn't faze him, though.

There's a life philosophy in there somewhere I'm a tad envious of.

I see Ellie before she sees me.

She's bounding out with Mikki, both giggling at who knows what.

Wait until she sees what's waiting in the car for her. I give Wilbur's back a pat. "She's going to love you, mate. A new family..."

I trail off, my chest tightening.

The reality of what I've done suddenly hits me, not like a ton of bricks but like a dump truck's worth. I adopted a dog. I brought a living creature into our little family of two, I introduced a new family member. And I did it without letting Ellie be involved.

Ah shit. Shit. I fucked up. She should have been a part of this. I should have—

Ellie sees my car. Then me. Like always, her face lights up when she sees me, which makes my *world* light up. God, I *live* for this little bag of mischief. She grins and waves with the hyper enthusiasm only a seven-year-old can have and starts running.

And stops.

Freezes.

Her stare is locked on Wilbur—who has decided to make this introduction all the more public by hanging so far out the passenger-side window I can hear the claws of his one front paw scraping on the door's paint.

Her eyes grow wide. Her mouth falls open.

She blinks.

Mikki comes up beside her, a small frown on her face, and asks a question: what's going on?

Ellie's lips move. Mikki looks at me. No, at *Wilbur*. Her eyebrows shoot up.

And Ellie is running again.

Straight for the car. Her stare locked on Wilbur.

"Love at first sight, mate?" I whisper, giving the seat he's standing on a little tap.

He looks at me over his shoulder, tail wagging, and turns back to look out the window, the immediate second Ellie reaches the car.

"You have a *dog*!" she exclaims from the kerb. She gapes up at Wilbur. "There's a dog in the car, Daddy."

Wilbur wags his tail harder.

And harder.

And loses balance and topples off the passenger seat onto the floor.

"Where'd he go?" Ellie giggles.

Wilbur bounds back up onto the seat, and once again, is straining out of the passenger window. Thank God for the car harness I bought at the shelter, otherwise he'd be out the window.

Behind me, someone with no time for this love-at-first-sight moment, beeps their horn.

Wilbur scurries back into the seat, almost landing on my lap.

I jump, shooting the person behind me a scowl in the rear-vision mirror.

A man wearing wraparound sunglasses sitting behind the wheel of a Tesla waves an impatient hand at me. "Hurry up," he says. At least, I think that's what he says.

Glancing straight ahead, I realise we're not fourth in line now, but first.

"Quick, kiddo," I call to Ellie.

No need. She's already flinging open the passenger door and scrambling in. "There's a dog in the car, Daddy," she repeats, the words almost lost in her laugh.

Wilbur presses into my side. I can feel him trembling.

I remember the way he cowered behind the bars back in the shelter, the way he tucked his tail when I moved at him too fast when he took Byron.

I want to find the person who mistreated him and—

Ellie pulls the door shut with a solid thud, throws her school backpack into the backseat, and stares at Wilbur.

Wilbur trembles more, pressing harder to my side.

I did not think this through. At all.

"Whose dog, Daddy? Why does he only have three legs? He's so cute. Where did he come from? What happened to his other leg? Can I pat him? Can I hold him while we drive?"

The questions fall from her so quickly, words tumble over each other. I want to answer them all.

Sunglasses beeps his Tesla's horn again.

Yeah, yeah. Hold your horses.

"His name is Wilbur," I say gently. "And if you promise to stay very still and quiet and calm, he can sit on your lap for a second. But just a second, and then you have to get into your seat in the back so we can drive home, okay?"

Her eyes grow to the size of saucers. She sits up so straight it's a wonder her spine doesn't snap, and nods fiercely.

"I can do that," she whispers, smoothing her palms over the tops of her legs, flattening the material of her school uniform's skirt.

Sunglasses beeps again.

I very gently coax Wilbur off my side and encourage him onto Ellie's lap.

I have no freaking clue if I'm doing the right thing or not.

Maybe I should have read a book about owning a dog before getting one? Maybe I should have asked Chelsea to come with me for this?

Yep, I'm freaking out.

And then Ellie giggles and I realise Wilbur is on her lap, enthusiastically licking her face.

"I love him," she declares. "I love him so much."

And just like that, my family has grown to three.

Sunglasses beeps behind me again.

As an environmentalist, I applaud his choice in car; as a father who just changed everything for his daughter, well, the guy needs to take a chill pill.

I smile at Ellie. "Quick, hop into the backseat. You can hug Wilbur to your heart's content when we get home."

Ellie beams, and scrambles over the centre console into the back, climbing into her booster seat. "Let's go," she giggles, buckling up.

I put my car into gear and pull away.

CHELSEA

I SHOULDN'T BE NERVOUS.

He's just a prospective new client. Nothing more.

It seems the horde of ADHD butterflies in my stomach didn't get the memo though.

I check the address Tim had texted me five hours ago, even though I don't need to. I know I'm in front of his apartment building. I've returned to the scene of the crime. In fact, is that dried pineapple juice on the concrete directly in front of the building's entry foyer?

The butterflies ramp up their party in my stomach. Rave levels activated.

I picture a butterfly net.

"Just a prospective new client," I muttered, picturing that net capturing a cloud of ADHD butterflies. "That's all."

Pressing the security button for his apartment number, I draw in a deep breath.

"Are you Chelsea?" a little girl's voice asks behind me.

The breath I'd just pulled in bursts from me in a startled cough as I spin around. The recently captured butterflies run amuck again.

Tim is standing a few feet away, his daughter—Ellie—perched on his shoulders, his arm extended as he grips a straining lead. And at the end of the lead is the scruffiest dog I've ever seen.

Wilbur.

Wilbur's whole body is quivering and wobbling, he's almost dancing on the spot on the end of the lead, his stubby tail is lashing side to side, and it takes my kerfuffled brain a few seconds to notice he only has one front leg.

Did Tim tell me that before?

I take a gentle step toward the excited dog and slowly lower myself into a crouch in front of him, and extend my hand, palm down, fingers slack, towards him. "I am Chelsea." I smile up at Ellie, letting Wilbur take his time to decide if he wants to sniff my hand or not. "You must be Ellie."

A wide smile splits her little face, and she wriggles a little on Tim's shoulders. "I *am* Ellie. I remember you from this morning. You spilt juice on Daddy. And knocked him onto his butt."

Tim laughs.

I pull an embarrassed face. "I did do that." I lower my

attention to Wilbur, who hasn't quite yet touched his nose to the back of my fingers, but it's close.

They probably smell like Gary. Or dog treats. Or both.

"And this is Wilbur," I say gently.

His semi-tucked tail is swiping side-to-side in nervous little swipes.

"Isn't he *awesome*!?" Ellie proclaims.

Looking up, I see Tim is gripping one of her legs with white-knuckled fingers to keep her steady, as she beams down at Wilbur. I love her already.

I mean, I don't have any right to love her, but she's as adorable as her three-legged dog.

"How long have you had him for?" I ask her with a smile. Because she's awesome and because Wilbur's cool, wet nose is kissing my fingers. Yes. A good sign.

Ellie's fair eyebrows shoot up. "Only since—"

"Shall we ask Chelsea inside?" Tim interrupts, looking up at Ellie as best as he can, given she's on his shoulders. "We can open the Tim Tams if she'd like one?"

"Tim Tams?" Ellie grabs at his hair and bends over his head. "Really, really? Before dinner?"

Tim laughs, shooting me a wry smile. And yep, I've fallen in love with him already as well.

Well, not literally but whoa...I could.

Seriously, I could.

"Let's go in—" I'm about to say *side* when Wilbur plants his front leg—singular—smack-bam on the middle of my chest and knocks me on my butt.

"Oh my God," Tim bursts out, as Wilbur starts licking my face with doggy enthusiasm. "I'm sorry." He starts laughing, tugging on Wilbur's lead. "But...but c'mon, karma, right?"

Karma is right.

Laughing, I gently return Wilbur's front foot to the sidewalk and climb to my feet. Let's see what we're working with here. I look at him, hold my right hand up, palm out. "Wilbur, sit."

He does. Instantly and perfectly.

"Heya, look at that!" Pride fills Tim's voice as he admires his dog's sit. "Well done, mate." He shoots me a smile and the butterflies try to start up the rave in my stomach again. "You *are* good."

The compliment does things to me a simple, unearned compliment about my dog-training skills shouldn't do.

I may not be in love with Timothy Holt yet, but I'm sure as hell in *lust* with him.

"Not me." Smiling, I give Wilbur a pat as a reward. "That's all Wilbur." My treat pouch—full of training treats—is still in my backpack. I usually put it on before knocking on the client's door, but because I was stupidly thinking about what Tim would see when he first opened his door, I didn't this time.

I need to get my head back on task.

Me, dog trainer. Him, dog owner. And possible client. And *way* out of my league. Even if he has kind of-sort of asked me to dinner tomorrow night. God, what am I going to wear?

Focus. Focus.

Tim smiles at me, and I have to stop myself blurting out how nice I think his eyes are.

I smile back.

He suddenly draws in a deep breath.

He's looking at me. His eyes are holding mine. I feel them all the way to my soul. I swallow.

"Daddy, are you doing a staring contest with Chelsea?" Ellie asks.

Tim blinks.

I do as well. Heat fills my cheeks.

Okay, that was some intense eye-contact there. I'm not

imagining it. He was looking at me and I was looking at him and maybe Marjory was right? Maybe he *is* interested in me? Maybe he does want to eat me up like a warm croissant? Maybe this is something that could actually...

Wilbur jumps up on me again, his front paw pressing at the top of my right thigh. His timing is perfect. I need to stop being deluded about Tim and focus on training Wilbur. That's why I'm here. To help Tim and Ellie and Wilbur.

"Wilbur," I say, putting on my best I-am-a-brilliant-dog-trainer voice. "Sit."

He does, stumpy tail wagging.

Tim laughs. "Can you move in?"

My heart slams into my throat and I look at him.

His Adam's apple jerks up and down his throat and he lets out another laugh, this one very wobbly. "Let's head inside."

We head inside.

T *im*

OKAY, so Chelsea Parker is in my home.

Not gonna lie; it feels...right.

Ellie is smitten. She gazes up at her like she's the second coming. It probably has something to do with Chelsea's amazing hair. Ellie has a thing for hair, and Chelsea's is a tousled tumble of glossy dark waves that fall around her face and down her shoulders and her back.

It might also have to do with the fact that, unlike a lot of adults that come and go in Ellie's life, Chelsea doesn't ignore her or talk to her like she's a baby. So many of the adults in my circle think the best way to deal with Ellie since Belinda's death is to pretend she's a fragile child. Ellie isn't. Ellie is feisty and funny and has more resilience than most of the adults I know.

In the first fifteen minutes of Chelsea being in our home, she focussed on Ellie and Wilbur as a combined unit.

Ellie listened to every word with intense concentration as Chelsea talked with her about what Wilbur's body language was saying, nodding often, answering questions, giggling whenever Chelsea told her she was awesome.

Chelsea told Ellie she was awesome often.

I think *Chelsea* is awesome, but I'm not sure I'm allowed to tell her that. Would that be pushing things too fast? Holy hell, it's been so long since I experienced this...this...core-deep interest I actually don't know what to do with—

"Wilbur!"

Ellie's squealing laughter yanks me out of my confusing thoughts and I turn from where I'm meant to be making me and Chelsea a cup of tea, but where I was instead pondering this strange path my life seems to be taking.

"Daddy!" Ellie is staring at me, horrified. "Wilbur is *weeing* on the coffee table."

Wilbur is, indeed, cocking his leg on the coffee table.

"Oh, no," Chelsea gasps from the dining table. She seems to be fastening a pouch of some sort around her waist.

Wilbur finishes evacuating his bladder, sniffs his achievement, and then trots over to her, tail wagging.

"Ummm." I freeze. The coffee table is a steel and glass number, but the woollen rug beneath it was an engagement present to me and Belinda from the *then* prime minister of New Zealand.

Ellie crinkles up her nose.

Chelsea gives Wilbur a gentle pat on his head. "Do you have a bucket? And some old towels?" Her voice is that same serious but calm tone she used to get him to sit. "I'm sorry. I was putting on my training pouch and didn't notice. Is he toilet trained?"

I have no freaking clue. Probably something I should have asked back at the shelter. On the short walk Ellie and I just took him on, he peed on almost every streetlight, street sign, blade of grass, and pebble we passed. How big is his bladder? "I—"

"I'll get the bucket and towels!" Ellie declares, as if she's announcing she's going to retrieve the fabled Ark of the Covenant, before running from the living room toward the laundry.

"It could be a stress thing," Chelsea says, dropping into a crouch to scratch at Wilbur's ears. "How does he normally respond to new people in your home?"

A disquieting knot twists in my gut. "You're the first new person he's met here."

Why am I reluctant to tell her Wilbur only joined my family today? It's a pretty important piece of information.

Because there's a part of you that acknowledges the initial reason for a dog being in your house is a selfish one, a self-serving one, and you don't want Chelsea to know that?

A finger of guilt slithers up my spine.

"Well, I'm honoured," Chelsea says, and it takes me a few seconds to remember what she's honoured about. Not me adopting a dog to meet a girl, but her being Wilbur's first house guest.

"He's a cool dog," I say, because I don't actually know what else to say at that point. And he is, indeed, a cool dog, regardless of his reckless peeing choices.

Wilbur wags his tail, looking at me from Chelsea's knees.

"A very cool dog." She smiles and instantly I smile back. "And a very smart one. Once we clean up his pee, we can see how he goes with the basics. We know he has sit down pat. Is there anything in particular you're worried about?"

You finding out I'm a sham dog owner.

"He seems to like Lord Byron a bit too much."

She blinks. Frowns.

"Ellie's favourite teddy bear," I clarify. Yeah, I'm an idiot. A distracted idiot. "Today I had to retrieve Bryon from Wilbur's mouth."

She lets out a soft chuckle and turns her smile to Wilbur. "Ah, we don't want to have teddy-bear guts strewn all over the living room. That's a tragic crime scene to be sure."

Wilbur makes an attempt to jump up on her again and she does this little move with her head—a little turn away—as she straightens to her feet, hands behind her back. He looks up at her, his body quivering, his stare locked on her, and then, suddenly sits.

"Yes," she says with a grin, withdrawing something from the pouch on her waist and giving it to him. "That's what I'm wanting." She looks up at me. "That's going to be your marker word for training. Y-E-S. When Wilbur does what you're asking him to do, or he does what you want from him without being asked, you say the marker word and reward him with a treat."

"Okay," I say.

She flicks him a glance, nods when he doesn't try to jump up on her again, and dips her hand into her pouch again. "Yes," she says, giving him another treat, followed by a quick pat on the back of the head. "You're a smart boy, aren't you?"

"Yes." I beam, proud of him. "He is."

He wags his tail and hurries over to me.

"Try not to say the marker word unless you're going to give him a reward treat," Chelsea says, following. She hands me a few flat blackish shapes, and I have to stop myself sucking in a breath as her fingers brush my palms. Jesus, anyone would think I'm a fifteen-year-old boy.

Swallowing, I look down at Wilbur.

Who immediately jumps up at me, tail wagging.

"Turn your head and back," she instructs. "We're letting

him know this is not the behaviour we like without breaking his heart."

"It's breaking my heart," I say on a wobbly laugh as I turn away from Wilbur. In my head, I see him cowering in the shelter cage. I see his desperate need for love.

Wilbur's front paw collides with the back of my thighs a few times as he tries to get my attention and then...

Nothing.

"Now, turn," Chelsea says, and I can't help but feel happy at the approval in her voice, "say the marker word and give him a treat."

I turn.

Gazing up at me, Wilbur wags his tail. He quivers a little, as if preparing to launch himself off the floor again, and then... stays put.

"Yes!" I almost crow, before giving him one of the treats in my hand. And another. And another.

Chelsea laughs. "We'll have you trained quick smart."

I laugh, and scratch Wilbur behind the ear. "Hear that, mate. We'll have you trained quick smart."

Chelsea laughs again, and there's a quality to it that makes all the blood in my lower body hightail it to my cock. Christ, it's a mischievous laugh. It makes me so fucking horny. "I meant Wilbur and I will have *you* trained quick smart."

I lift my attention from Wilbur to her.

Our eyes connect. Hold.

She smiles and all the blood left in my body heads south.

Fuck. I want to kiss her so much, my breath catches in my throat.

And I think, I *think*, she might be feeling the same—

"Bucket!" Ellie sprints back into the room, waving the bucket, a towel flapping behind her from where she's tied it around her neck like a cape.

Wilbur cowers, ears dropped, and scurries around behind my legs. Yep, that's a little puddle of pee at my feet.

"Ellie," I chide, making sure I don't shout. She didn't know. "Shhh."

Dropping the bucket, she jolts to a stop, worried eyes looking at Wilbur before she swings them to Chelsea. "I didn't mean to make him wee. I'm sorry. I'm sorry. I'll be a good doggie owner. Please don't take him—"

"Hey, hey, hey," Chelsea murmurs, sinking down to a crouch, her smile warm and gentle as she looks at Ellie. "It's okay, munchkin. I would *never* take your puppy from you. I can see you're an amazing doggie owner. Don't stress, sweetie. It's okay."

"I scared him," Ellie says, the words a low mumble. "He weed."

Chelsea nods, her smile still gentle. "He did. But you and me and your dad are going to help Wilbur not be worried about sudden noises and surprises and before you know it, the only time he'll be weeing is when he sees a tree or street sign outside."

Ellie looks at Wilbur. At me. At Chelsea. "Promise?"

"Promise." Chelsea straightens, holding out her hand. "Now, I hear there's someone very special in your life called Lord Bryon? Can I meet him? While your dad cleans up Wilbur's little accidents?"

Ellie's smile lights up the world, and she grabs Chelsea's hand. "C'mon. Bryon's in my room!"

"We'll be back." Chelsea grins to me over her shoulder as Ellie starts dragging her from the living room. "Have fun with the pee."

And just like that, I'm pretty certain I'm one hundred percent in love with her.

I look down at Wilbur, who's inching his way out from behind my legs, tail wagging. "What am I going to do, mate?"

His answer—to wag his tail faster—is dubious advice, but I'll take it. Be happy, that tail says.

And I am. Even if I do have to now clean up two puddles of pee, without a towel, because Ellie is still wearing it.

I hurry into the kitchen, grab the roll of paper towel from under the sink, run some hot water into the bucket and then hurry back to the rug first. The chances of the ex-New Zealand PM ever coming to visit are slim, but it'd probably be better if there's no evidence the rug has been peed on.

My phone rings as I'm about to lower myself to my knees, a wad of paper towel in hand.

Lyle.

Shit.

I've ignored him all day.

If I ignore him for any longer, he's either going to turn up at my door, or Dad is. And I'm not in the mood for either of them. I'm too happy.

Pulling my phone from my back pocket, I accept the call and clunk onto the floor on my knees. Poor knees. "Lyle. Sorry I haven't got back to you today. Been a bit busy."

"We don't have to worry about the dog trainer after all," he says. "She's not a threat."

I blanch. Frown. The dog trainer? Chelsea? Does he know she's here? Does he know about Wilbur? Am I all over social media again? Did the shelter worker rat me out? Did the Uber driver? No, not Anton? Surely? "I have no clue what you're talking about."

"I was worried she was going to be a complication," he said, brisk as always. "The kind that could derail our plans and impact how voters perceive you, but it turns out that's not the case."

How voters *perceive* me? What the hell does Chelsea have to do with how voters perceive me?

"I truly have no idea—"

"She's already got a partner," he says, as if I haven't uttered a word. "Already in a relationship. So we can stop worrying she's going to become a problem."

Something cold creeps up the back of my neck and over my scalp. Already in a *relationship*?

No. Surely not.

There's no way I've misconstrued the way she's looked at me. The...the...spark between us. No way. Is there?

"That can't be—"

"Anyways," Lyle cuts me off. "Now that worry is behind us, I have a nine o'clock booked tomorrow for you with a Cavoodle breeder. Her prize bitch—who won Best in Show at this year's Sydney Royal Easter Championship—has just given birth to a litter and I've secured you a—"

"I've already got a dog," I announce. "His name is Wilbur. He has only three legs and he is awesome."

"You *what*?"

I end the call without answering. Rude, yes. But necessary. For my sanity.

My chest tightens, and a rough sigh bursts from me.

Relationship?

Wilbur sticks his cold, wet nose in my face. The ubiquitous tongue follows.

"Turn away, Tim."

Chelsea's calm voice startles me, and I jolt kind of upright, kind of backward.

Wilbur scurries after me, targeting my face, as if worried I didn't notice him trying to slather it in dog slobber a second ago.

"Turn away, Tim," Chelsea repeats.

Ellie giggles. "Doggy kisses!"

Instead of doing what my instincts tell me to do, which is laugh and gently push Wilbur away, I turn my head away from Wilbur.

I expect him to jump all over my back in a valiant effort to get his point across—hey, hey, I'm here, I'm here, I want to lick your face, I want to lick your face.

A few seconds of nothing, and I turn—carefully—back.

Wilbur is sitting and looking at me.

"Who's a good boy?" Chelsea murmurs.

I look at her, my heart fast. *Me*, I want to say. *I'm a good boy. Please love me instead.*

Holy shit, I'm in deep trouble here.

I think...I think I've bloody well gone and fallen in love with her. Already.

CHELSEA

THIS IS NOT how my discovery session is meant to go.

For starters, I'm meant to be *discovering* what issues the prospective new client's *dog* has. Instead, I'm discovering I like Tim Holt and Tim Holt's daughter way more than I should.

I'm also discovering Wilbur is pretty freaking incredible. Gary would love him. I can see them playing together in the park without any difficulty at all. I can see them snuggling up together at night, enjoying each other's warmth...

Or is that me and Tim snuggling up together?

I need to get out of here. Before I do or say something stupid. *Will you marry me?* That kind of stupid.

Besides, I should have left thirty minutes ago. My actual hour is up. The fact I have no client booked for the rest of the night doesn't help. Makes it so much easier to just...stay. Nor does the fact that Ellie—the adorable munchkin I know is already stealing my heart—keeps showing me awesome things from her room. Like the awesome drawing she's done of her dad being some kind of superhero wearing a green cape. Or her awesome pet rock with googly eyes and a glitter feather stuck on its back. And most of all, Lord Byron, her awesome and clearly well-loved teddy bear.

Wilbur also seems to like Byron. The second she ran out with the bear, Wilbur leapt to his three feet from where he was sitting beside Tim on the sofa, ran over, and snatched Byron from her hands.

There were squeals of protest.

There were tears of dismay.

There was a very excited dog with a very excited tail zooming around the apartment with Byron dangling from his mouth.

There was a very stressed—but still very sexy—Tim chasing a very excited dog around the apartment, doing everything wrong trying get Byron back.

And then, there was me.

Dog-trainer voice activated, treat pouch employed, I brought the chaos to an end.

Sort of.

"Oh God, I love you," Tim said as I handed Byron back to Ellie. His eyes locked on mine, and I almost believed he meant it.

"I love you too," Ellie declared, hugging her teddy with asphyxiating glee. She glared at Wilbur. "Bad Wilbur."

Wilbur tucked his tail. Peed a little.

"Oh, I'm *sorry*, Wilbur," Ellie had wailed, running at him, arms wide and ready for the hug Wilbur was in no way ready for.

And chaos began again.

I calmed it all down, did some incidental owner training, and now...well, now we're sitting at the dining table with glasses of water in our hands, and a plate of Tim Tams in front of us, as if we're a family, and Ellie is asking if I would like to stay for dinner.

Yeah, I should have left ages ago. This is just downright dangerous for my fragile state of mind. It's far too easy to imagine doing this every evening. The only thing missing is Gary.

"Can we get fish and chips, Daddy?" Ellie asks, sitting up straighter in her seat, her eyes wide. "Or pizza? Or...or...oh, can we get Thai? We haven't had Thai for ages." She turns those big eyes on me. "I love Thai. Do you like Thai? Moneybags are the best. Can Wilbur eat Thai?"

"Thai's probably not a good fit for Wilbur," I say. "What's his favourite food?"

A frown pulls at Ellie's eyebrows, and she opens her mouth.

"You are more than welcome to stay," Tim says. "If you like."

As if on cue, Wilbur rests his chin on my thigh, looking up at me with the dictionary definition of puppy-dog eyes.

So easy. So easy to say yes.

"I have to go," I say instead, giving Wilbur a soft pat before gently rising to my feet.

Something flickers across Tim's face. Something...confusing. Does he *want* me to stay for dinner? Does he actually *like* me? *Like* like me? Or is he just being an awesome single dad to his daughter?

"Oh, poo," Ellie declares, slumping. She then immediately sits up straight. "Can *we* still get Thai, Daddy?"

I chuckle, even as every fibre in my body screams at me to sit my arse right back down and pretend I'm Tim's girlfriend.

"Maybe," Tim murmurs, also rising to his feet. He's still watching me with that confusing gaze, and I wish to hell I was better at reading people. Animals, no worries. Dogs? I'm an expert. But people? Nope. It comes with a/ being a bit of an introvert who grew up with an introvert single-mum, and b/... okay, there's not really a b. I'm good at dogs. That's pretty much it.

Scooping up my treat pouch where I placed it on the sofa in the living room, my heart trying to beat its way out of my chest, I smile at them both. And pat Wilbur when he crosses to me. "I will make up some notes about our plan of attack for Wilbur and email them to you," I say as I head to the apartment's door. *Keep it professional, Chelsea. Don't be deluded.*

Tim follows. "Or conversely," he says, a warm laugh in his voice, "you could just give it to me tomorrow night."

Tomorrow night. Oh, my giddy aunt, tomorrow night. I'd forgotten. I'm going out to dinner with him tomorrow night to Angus's restaurant, with the intention of doing everything we basically did this evening.

I really should tell him there's no need anymore.

I really should.

Except he called me and asked me to dinner at Buckley's Chance, the most awarded and prestigious restaurant in the country, when he could have asked any of the important, beautiful, significant people in his social circle. But he asked me.

So even though I have to get out of here now before I completely let myself believe there's some fairy-tale romance brewing between us, I'm not above taking a second bite out of the biscuit and going to dinner with him at Angus's restaurant.

Besides, if I do, maybe...just maybe...I might mention

Marjory to him. And maybe, just maybe, he might be okay with me arranging for her to meet him.

And maybe, just maybe, she mightn't destroy my business with one Instagram post.

"Tomorrow night." I smile, giving him a nod. I hope I'm coming across as confident and maybe a little sexy and seductive, but I suspect it's more shy and awkward.

Ellie looks at both of us with high eyebrows. "What's happening tomorrow night?"

"Chelsea and I are going to dinner."

Yeah, my heart goes a bit mental at *that* sentence.

Ellie's eyebrows rise higher. "Ohhh, Dad and Chelsea sitting in a tree," she sing-songs. "Kay-eye—"

"Uh uh." Tim shakes his head, laughing, holding up a finger. "No. No."

Ellie giggles.

Tim throws a smile at me and my heart slams so hard up into my throat I almost hiccup. God, he's gorgeous.

"I've got to go," I say. "Bye."

And before another word can be uttered by either of them, I turn and damn near run from his apartment.

Not my proudest moment. Definitely not my most professional either.

But then, I am going to dinner with him tomorrow night in my brother's restaurant because my brother used his reputation to get Tim there with the entire plan of setting us up.

So yeah, situation normal?

Good grief, is it too late to reset the day?

9

T *im*

ONE OF US scared her off and I don't think it was Ellie or Wilbur.

"I like her," Ellie declares, even as she plonks down beside Wilbur and cheerfully accepts his kisses all over her face.

"Me too," I admit.

Ellie studies me, something going through her young mind I have no hope of deciphering, and raises her eyebrows again. "Thai?"

"Hmm," I say, pretending to contemplate it. Of course we're having Thai. "What about mushroom soup in—"

From somewhere in the living room comes the soft sound of Nick Blackthorne singing 'Gotta Run'.

I frown. An awesome song, to be sure, but one that has no right playing softly in my living room. When I play Blackthorne, I play it loud.

"You hear that?" I ask Ellie.

"I hear singing," she confirms, and then goes back to giving Wilbur her full attention.

Frowning some more, I straighten to my feet and go looking for the source of the epic rock ballad.

And find it.

There, on one of the sofas in my living room, is Chelsea Parker's backpack. Nick Blackthorne is singing from inside it.

If this is her phone ringer, I'm in even more danger of falling in love. Can't go wrong with Nick Blackthorne music. Ever.

Falling in love? She's supposedly got a partner, remember?

Maybe I can make her forget all about that partner. Maybe she'll realise she's not with the right partner after dinner tomorrow night?

For a second, just a second, I contemplate opening her bag and seeing who's calling her. Maybe even answer the call. Find out who this partner is and—

Oh my fucking God, what am I doing? I mean, I worried about how a life in politics might affect my moral compass, but holy shit, I'm not even officially sworn into the business and here I am being an absolute jerk? Invading a woman's privacy? Because I like her? Because I'm horny?

I take a step back and swipe my hand over my mouth.

Nick Blackthorne stops singing.

My blood roars in my ears. I stare at her bag. I feel... unsettled.

And then I realise I'm standing in my living room staring at Chelsea's bag when only a few moments ago she left.

Jesus, take it down to her, idiot. Now!

I snatch up her bag and hurry for the door. "Els, stay put," I instruct, pointing at her. "Chelsea forgot her bag."

I swing open the door.

"Okay, Daddy."

Wilbur is at my side by the time I've stepped across the threshold. For a second, I consider putting him back inside with Ellie, but the cautious—i.e.: over-protective—father in me remembers I have no clue of his history and I'm not ready to leave my seven-year-old daughter unsupervised with him. Yet.

We hurry down the stairs. Quicker than taking the lift.

I'm holding onto Chelsea's bag like it's a life raft.

Nick Blackthorne starts singing from inside it again.

Again, I want to see who it is.

Again, I do my best to ignore the lure, grateful for the first time ever when Blackthorne shuts up.

Arriving at ground level, I sling her bag over my shoulder, and half-bend inelegantly to hook my finger under Wilbur's collar. The last thing I want is for him to run off.

That'd break Ellie's heart *and* mine.

We cross the building's foyer and burst out onto the footpath.

The early evening summer breeze flows around us, bringing with it the salty harbour air and the sweet smell of eucalyptus and jasmine. It's a beautiful night for a walk and for a potent second an image of me, Chelsea, Ellie, and Wilbur strolling together along the harbour's edge slams into my mind. Chelsea's holding my hand. Ellie's holding her other. I'm holding Wilbur's leash.

It steals my breath and I let out a weird grunt.

God, I'm in—

Wilbur lurches against my awkward hold on his collar, and I know he's seen Chelsea before me thanks to the frenzied tail-wagging wobbling his body side to side.

I look in the direction he's trying to drag me, and yep, there she is, standing beside a VW beetle that looks like it's seen better days, her forehead resting on her forearms as she leans against it.

Is she okay?

Wilbur lets out an excited single bark and she startles, snapping her head my way.

Great, stealth mode shattered.

She jerks away from the car, smoothing her palms over her chest, her thighs, through her hair, and shakes her head, smiling at me.

She seems as unsettled as I am. Maybe I really do stand a chance?

Stop it.

"You forgot your bag," I say as Wilbur drags me to her.

She frowns at me for a heartbeat and then pats the front of her shoulder, frowning at it. "Oh God, I did too." She turns back to me, the smile I'm getting seriously used to back on her face. "Thank you."

I hand over her bag. Reluctantly.

There are many, many things I want to know about her. Like, what's her favourite movie, her favourite book? Does she like sailing? Does she like camping? Where does she stand on pineapple on pizza? What're her thoughts on ice cream? Picnics? Climate change? Is she already in a relationship and if not, would she like to be?

If she gets in her car and drives away now, I'll have to wait to tomorrow night to find out.

I don't want to wait.

Do you have a partner?

Thankfully, I bite back the question before I blurt it out.

"I think someone's been trying to call you," I say instead, pointing at her bag. "Nick Blackthorne has been playing in there."

Another quick frown before she laughs. "Ahh, was it 'Gotta Run'?"

"Yeah."

"I love that song," she says as she digs her phone out of her bag.

"Me too," I say, trying not to sneak a glance at her phone's screen.

Chewing on her lip, she swipes her thumb over her phone's screen, taps something out, and then shoves her phone back in her bag and smiles at me. "Thank you. For bringing it down." She drops into a crouch and gives Wilbur at scratch behind both his ears. "You're a good boy."

Straightening, she meets my gaze. "If you let him go, will he run away? Do we need to work on recall?"

"I don't—" *Know*. I stop myself saying *know*. As a loving, responsible dog owner, I *should* know that. My stomach knots. "Playing it safe," I say. "Just in case."

"Hmm." She looks at Wilbur. "Wilbur, sit."

He does.

"Yes!" She dips her hand into the treat pouch she's still wearing around her waist and gives him one.

Wilbur wags his tail.

"Thank you." Her eyes find mine again and I just want to fall into them. "Again. I'll see you tomorrow night? At the restaurant?"

"I'll pick you up." I'm turning this into a date. I can't help myself. It dawns on me she never actually said yes to me picking her up when I first asked her on the phone earlier today.

She studies me, her expression unreadable.

Surely if she says yes to me picking her up, she doesn't have a partner? Right?

"I'll meet you there," she finally says. "If that's okay?"

A heavy weight crushes my chest.

Her smile is...shy? "It'll save you trying to get across the city at that crazy hour to get me."

I don't mind. Not at all.

"Sure." I nod. "See you then."

She pulls out her keys, opens her car door, and, after throwing her bag into the front passenger seat, removes her treat pouch and then slides into the seat behind the wheel.

I scoop Wilbur up into my arms—my spine is not enjoying the constant awkward angle I'm forcing on it—and take a step back.

Her eyes find mine again, her expression still unreadable, and she closes the door.

The engine of the VW clicks.

And nothing else.

Just a click.

Chelsea squeezes her eyes shut and turns the key in the ignition again.

Another click.

And only a click.

I compress my lips and give Wilbur a little jiggle. I'm not happy her car isn't starting. I'm not.

Bullshit.

After five more clicks, she gets out of her car, cheeks red. "Well, this is embarrassing."

I let out a chuckle. "Fossil-fuel driven cars, eh? What good are they?"

She laughs.

"How 'bout I drive you home?" The offer is out, hanging in the air between us, before I realise I've even formed the words. I try to recover by giving her a cheesy grin. "I'm definitely cheaper than a rideshare."

She opens her mouth. Closes it. Opens it again.

I want to follow the unexpected offer with *Please*. Or *it's not a problem*. Or *how about you just stay here?*

A smile plays with her lips, and my heart beats out a happy rhythm. "Okay."

Yes. This is good. More time with her.

"I'll call... I'll call my brother and get him to help me collect it later," she continues, chewing on her bottom lip. "I just want to get home to Gary."

A tight finger of something hot and unbecoming slides up my back. Who's Gary? Her partner? The one Lyle said Chelsea had? But if that's the case, why wouldn't Gary help her out with her car? Unless Gary can't drive? Maybe Gary doesn't have his licence? Maybe he lost it after a DUI? I've never lost my licence with a DUI. I should point that out.

Oh my fucking God, what is wrong with me?

Self-loathing crawls over my scalp in a pricking heat. "Give me a sec and I'll go ask my neighbour if Ellie can go hang out with her for a bit," I say, adjusting Wilbur in my arms.

Before she can reply, and before I say or do something stupid, I hurry back inside.

Wilbur licks my face the whole way.

It takes me barely a minute to get Ellie down to Mrs. Angelo. It didn't take either of them much convincing. The last time Ellie stayed a few hours with Mrs. Angelo, they spent over two-hundred dollars ordering everything they wanted from UberEats. Mrs. Angelo is determined to be the best surrogate grandmother Ellie has, and if achieving that mission requires copious amounts of junk food, then so be it.

On Mrs. Angelo's insistence, I leave Wilbur with them.

"I've owned three Rottweilers and a Doberman in my life, Timothy," she informs me as I begin to express concern. "I know dogs."

Wilbur wags his tail as I give him a pat and tell him to behave.

Ellie grins as I tell her not to eat too much rubbish.

Mrs. Angelo tuts as I tell her the same.

A minute later, I'm hurrying towards Chelsea where she's standing beside her dead car. She's texting someone, but looks up as I approach, and smiles.

That smile... That smile will be my demise.

"Thank you." She puts her phone back into her bag. "You really are saving me."

"Just call me your knight in..." I look down at what I'm wearing. "Jeans and a polo shirt."

She chuckles. I like the way it sounds. Relaxed. Warm.

Partnerless?

Fuck a duck, I need to get a grip.

CHELSEA

HE DRIVES A HYBRID VOLVO. Of course.

I'm nervous. Ridiculously nervous. Not because of his choice of car, but because we're in it, just the two of us, with no other forms of distractions or interruptions.

I'm in grave danger of babbling like an idiot.

Good grief, I'm nervous.

As we pull out of the parking level, I can't stop myself stealing glances at him.

He's concentrating on the road—we're right in the middle of insane peak-hour Sydney traffic—and that gives me the chance to surreptitiously check him out—as if I need to. I think I've already got his image burned into my brain.

There's a common belief in Australia, and maybe the world, that people with red hair can't be sexy. Hello? They clearly haven't met Timothy Holt. His dark coppery-red hair and dark-red eyebrows just highlight everything that is gorgeous about his face: his square jaw, complete with an insanely sexy ginger stubble, his hawkish nose, his expressive lips that are curled in a smile now even as he focuses on the crazy traffic.

I like looking at him.

I'm so confused by him.

I'm convinced we have a connection—good grief, I'm resorting to cliches—and I'm also convinced there's no way we have a connection and I'm imagining the whole thing.

I really should have just got an Uber, or called Angus to come get me, instead of letting Tim drive me home. It's going to take at least thirty minutes, depending on the traffic, and what can I possibly talk about in that time that'll interest him?

"So, favourite cheese?" he says suddenly, throwing me a grin. "Or colour. Take your pick."

"Blue," I reply, loving his relaxed and playful sense of humour.

"Is that colour, or cheese?"

"Both."

"Ha. I had you pegged more as a vintage cheddar person."

I raise my eyebrows.

"Y'know." He gives me another quick grin. "'Cause it's got bite. Bite? Dog trainer? Get it?"

I groan. He laughs. "Yeah, Ellie thinks my dad jokes suck as well. So tell me, how did you get into dog training?"

Before I can answer, his phone rings. The Volvo's CarPlay system tells us it's Sophie Patel from the New Zealand Crown Research Institute.

"Sorry." He pulls a face. "I've got to take this."

"Go for it."

Turns out I don't have to panic about what we'd talk about on the drive; he speaks to Sophie for fifteen minutes—mainly about windfarms in the Pacific Ocean—before an incoming call from—according to CarPlay—Ari from West Australia Renewable Consortium causes him to finish his conversation with Sophie and accept Ari's.

I tune the conversation out with a smile. I love how passionate he sounds when talking about renewable energy. I understand it. I get passionate when I talk about dogs.

We're a block from my place, when I hear Ari say, "Saw you on the TV this morning. Didn't think you could drop the F-bomb on a live breakfast show."

Tim groans.

Ari laughs. "Hey, it'll either help your planned political career, or destroy it before it starts."

He chuckles this time. "I'm sure there's a focus group out there already at work deciding the answer."

Political career? Is he thinking of going into politics? I guess he's following in his father's footsteps, but still...a politician?

"And I'm also told you're in some kind of relationship with a dog trainer," Ari says, although the question in his voice is clear.

My throat slams shut.

Tim shoots a look at me.

Our eyes hold. For much longer than they should, given he's driving.

Silence stretches between us.

And then, feeling braver than I ever have in my entire life, I cock an eyebrow at him and let my lips curl into a smile that says—I hope—*I'm game if you are.*

A muscle bunches in his jaw.

Ah crap. *Crap*, why did I *do* that? Why did I *even* think doing that was a clever idea? He's the freaking ex-PM's son. He's way out of my league. He's Timothy freaking Holt, and I'm just a dog trainer with an alcoholic dead dad and a business loan that could sink me any day now. Why did I think it was a good idea to—

"Maybe," he says.

My heart launches up into my currently slammed-shut throat.

Maybe? Did he just say maybe? Okay, okay. Don't panic. Play it cool. Play it—

"I gotta go, Ari," he says, turning his attention back to the world outside the car. "I'll send those reports to you later tonight."

He ends the call just as we silently pull into my driveway.

There's a charged energy in the air. An unseen...something. My chest is tight. His jaw bunches. He presses a button on the dash—killing the Volvo's electric engine, maybe? I can't tell by the sound. His stare is locked on the darkening night on the other side of the windscreen.

"I—" I begin even though I have zero clue what I'm intending to say.

"Who's Gary?" he asks at the same time, twisting in his seat to pin me with eyes almost hidden in the evening's shadows.

I blink. Frown. "Gary? My dog."

He stares at me, motionless for a heartbeat, and then a choppy laugh falls from him. "Your dog. Phew. Okay. Your dog. Not your partner."

"My partner?" Confusion blooms through me. "Do you mean business partner? I don't have one."

"No, I mean..." he pauses for a second, waving a hand in the universally recognised *y'know* gesture. "*Partner.*"

"Oh." My eyes widen. "I don't have one of those either."

Relief rushes over his face.

Heat rushes over mine. The fact he's relieved I *don't* have a partner fills me with an excited little thrill.

"So Lyle was wrong." He lets out a soft grunt. "That's going to irritate him to no end. I can't wait to tell him."

"Lyle told you I had a partner?"

"Yes."

I can't stop my own laughing grunt. "Lyle came to see me today. My brother was visiting at the time."

"Lyle came to *see* you?" There's an edge to his voice. A steely one.

Oh, Lyle, you better watch out.

"At your *home*? Why?"

"I think to warn me off you." Oh God, did I really just say that?

He looks at me, his expression completely impossible to decipher. His nostrils flare. "That is completely out of order, and I'll be having a word with him about it. I'm so sorry."

"It's okay," I say, putting a hand on his forearm.

He freezes. Drops his stare to it.

I suck in a breath and pull my hand away.

His fingers catch mine, halting my hasty movement.

We stare at each other. My heart is pounding in my ears.

"I like you, Chelsea," he says, the words husky.

"I like you too," I confess. Oh boy. Oh boy. Oh boy. Is this happening? Is this—

He leans towards me.

I meet him in the middle.

Our lips crush and collide over the centre console, our hands burying in each other's hair. Our tongues...our tongues do things together my tongue hasn't done with another tongue for a long time.

Kissing. We're kissing. We're kissing each other. No, we're devouring each other. And it's so freaking good.

Oh.

My.

God.

10

T *im*

THERE'S a whole storm of emotions swirling through me at this very moment in time; lust, surprise, guilt, hope, lust, I said lust, right? need, hunger, fear, and lust. But the main emotion, the one in some semblance of control of the uncontrollable, is certainty.

This is right.

More than right.

Kissing Chelsea is right.

This is exactly what I am meant to be doing. I can feel it in my soul. It's not just a physical response, although I've got a hard-on so fucking, well, hard, it's excruciating, but it's not just my body, my cock, that approves.

My soul does.

My heart does.

And it's that realisation that stops me from kissing her like a horny, sex-starved fifteen-year-old. It's the realisation I want to kiss her many, many, *many* more times, in many, many more situations and places, and for many, many more reasons—not just lust.

I soften my assault on her lips and, with a tiny noise that makes me almost shoot my load there and then, Chelsea does the same.

Our lips explore each other now with a tenderness that makes my head spin. Our tongues, only a second ago wild and feverish, now touch and slide over each other with a reverence that rocks me to the core.

My head swims, or maybe it's the world that's spinning. Whatever it is, I need air. Almost as much as I need to keep kissing her.

Her fingers slip from my hair and feather over my jaw and a maelstrom of responses crash through me—carnal and soul deep. Fuck, I want her so much I'm on the verge of losing control.

I pull away, breath bursting from me in choppy pants.

She's watching me; I can feel her eyes on me in the darkness. The sun has completely disappeared behind the horizon since I pulled into her driveway.

"Umm..." she says.

I chuckle nervously. "That...that was good."

Good? Jesus, I used to be better at this. At least, I think I was. I was never a player.

Her own laugh is as nervous as mine. "It was."

I swallow. I'm hard. When was the last time I got a hard-on just from a kiss? Thank God, it's dark in the car.

"Would you like to come in and meet Gary?"

My cock throbs harder at her soft invitation. My balls do the same. Every fibre in my body screams yes.

Come in.

Come in.

Fuck.

"I can't," I ground out.

She lets out a soft sound that almost rips me apart. "Oh."

"I want to." I swallow again. My mouth is dry, and my dick is aching. "But if I go inside with you, into your house...I...I don't think I'd be able to keep my hands off you."

Soft fingers brush over my jaw again. "Isn't that the idea?"

I suck in a sharp breath. "Introduce me to Gary."

She flings open her car door, and for the fleeting second the interior light illuminates us both, I see a hunger in her eyes I recognise in my own core.

I don't know how I'm going to recover from this.

I don't care.

I scramble out of my Volvo, slam the door, hurry halfway up the driveway after her, remember I didn't lock my Volvo, hurry a quarter of the way back, think 'What the fuck am I doing? Chelsea is waiting!', hurry an eighth of the way back to her house, stop, drag in a breath.

Okay, I'm kind of freaking out.

I think...*think*...I'm about to make out with a gorgeous, sexy woman I met just over twelve hours ago. I haven't made out with a gorgeous, sexy woman in over a year and a half.

I haven't made out with anyone, period, for over a year and a half, gorgeous and sexy and female or not.

It's a huge fucking step. What does *making out* mean nowadays? What if I fuck it up?

"Tim?" Chelsea's soft voice calls from her front porch. Gentle and curious at once.

Pulling in a deep breath, I dig into my pocket, lock the Volvo with the keys from where I'm standing, and turn back to look up at her.

The front door light is on—no doubt a security sensor light —and she stands motionless, one hand on the doorknob.

She is gorgeous, a simple, natural beauty that steals my breath and makes my blood run hotter than it has in a long time.

I'm *not* going to fuck this up. There's *something* here, some-thing between us that is more significant than just a making out session. There's something special.

I like special. Just as much as I like her.

Steadying myself with another deep breath, I close the distance between us with sure strides and come to a stop in front of her.

She looks up at me, her teeth catching her bottom lip.

"If you're not ready," I say, "I understand. I want you. I'm not going to lie. It kind of scares the hell out of me how much I want you, but I don't want you to feel rushed. If you've changed your—"

She silences me with the kind of kiss that makes it very clear she hasn't changed her mind.

11

C *helsea*

THERE'S A TINY, tiny voice in my head screaming at me I'm kissing Tim Holt at my front door, under a light, where anyone walking or driving past can see.

I don't know if that voice is excited or worried.

All I know is I'm kissing Tim Holt. Again.

His lips and tongue move with mine and I can't stop the thoroughly horny groan vibrating in the back of my throat. This man makes me want to do filthy things to him.

And by the way his hands are buried in my hair, by the way his body is pressing to mine, filthy things are on his mind as well.

I am one hundred percent okay with that.

When my knees begin to tremble, I pull away, almost slumping against my door with a soft thud.

His nostrils flare as he studies me, wordless. I think we're both shocked.

Holding his gaze, I draw in a shaky breath, and then turn to unlock the door. As the key slides into the lock, he brushes my hair from the back of my neck and nibbles a little line of kisses over my skin.

I think I'm going to orgasm there and then.

His hands slip around my hips, and with gentle pressure, he draws me back to his body, the fingers of his right hand skimming up over my ribcage just under my left boob as the fingers of his left slip lower over my stomach. Lower still. Under the waistband of my jeans. Skin on skin. Toward my—

Enthusiastic barking bursts from the other side of the door and we both jump. Tim almost stumbles backward, like he's been busted doing something he shouldn't.

To hell with that. He should. Again. And again.

And again.

"That's Gary," I say, giving Tim a smile as I unlock the door. "Sorry. He's going to be very happy to see me."

"Totally understand," he says. "Can't blame him. I'm very happy to see you as well."

I don't miss the innuendo.

Neither does my body.

Holding his gaze, I open the door.

Gary—ever the good boy—greets me with a perfect sit and a tail wag just inside the door. "Heya, my big guy," I say, crouching down to give him a pat.

Detecting Wilbur's scent, Gary goes into sniffing overdrive.

I smile up at Tim, letting Gary explore my clothes with his nose. "This is Gary. He's old, but still awesome."

Tim crosses the threshold into my home, crouches down beside me, and gives Gary a gentle pat. "Hey, mate."

Gary licks his hand and my heart slams out of my chest.

It's not that I judge people by how they talk to dogs, how they treat animals, it's just...yeah, I judge people by how they talk to dogs and treat animals.

A few seconds ago, Tim and I were close to doing something on my front porch that would probably get us both arrested for public indecency. Now, Tim was patting my dog. He could have stepped past Gary, given what we *were* doing and what we're *planning* on doing and just strode into my living room and, after I got Gary settled, we would have continued where we let off. It's what Roger used to do.

But he didn't. He stopped and is now patting Gary. And Gary is licking his hand.

I wasn't prepared for this.

"He's an awesome dog," Tim says, smiling at Gary. "Did you get him as a puppy?"

I turn my attention to Gary, who is lapping up all the attention.

"Gary came into my life three years ago. A week after my mum passed away. Kara—my best friend—and I were planting a tree in the small front yard to remember her by, when Gary ambled in through the front gate and plonked himself on the grass next to us, tail wagging."

I watch Tim's hands gently scratch behind Gary's ears. I am one hundred percent falling in love with him, which is a huge problem but one I'll deal with later. Gary and I can eat a tub of ice cream to get over him when reality resumes, I guess.

"He had no collar, no microchip, and clearly hadn't had a bath in...well, a very long time," I continue, tracing my finger along the faint white line of fur running down one side of Gary's nose. "It was love at first sight. He filled the ache in my heart with unconditional love and I filled his belly with half the roast chicken I had in the fridge. And half the turkey meatloaf I'd made the night before." I let out a soft chuckle and lift my attention to Tim.

He's studying me.

"He found where he was meant to be," he says.

I nod, a sudden pressure wrapping around my chest.

"I think," Tim murmurs, his gaze holding mine, "I have as well."

Yeah, I'm in love.

I catch my lip with my teeth. It's all I can do to stop myself blurting it out. Or throwing myself at him.

He flicks Gary a quick look. "Is Gary going to be okay with me kissing you?" He looks at me. "Because I really want to kiss you again."

I straighten to my feet and toss my head towards the living room. "Gary, on your bed."

With a wag of his tail—and one final lick of Tim's hand—Gary trots over to his big, fluffy bed and flops onto it.

"Impressive." Tim stands, arching an eyebrow at me. "What happens if I say, 'Chelsea, on your bed.'?"

"Depends." I laugh, my pulse racing. "Are you going to give me a treat if I do?"

His nostrils flare. "Chelsea, on your bed."

I hold his gaze for a second, and then turn to Gary. "Gary, stay."

Gary wags his tail again and bunkers down, getting himself more comfortable in his bed.

Giving Tim an arched eyebrow of my own, I turn on my heel and walk to my bedroom. I think I'm doing my best sexy walk, but given I've never tried to do a sexy walk before, I may look like an idiot.

"Good boy, Gary," Tim says behind me.

I'm perched on the end of my bed, cross-legged, heart pounding, when he appears at the door.

He stops. His chest rises and falls with a deep, shaky breath.

"My treat?" I ask.

He digs his hand into his jeans pocket, withdraws a small chip of live treat—one of the ones I gave him back at his place, no doubt—and holds it up.

"Hmmm." I grin. "Not what I had in mind."

He chuckles. "And what did you have in—"

I pull my T-shirt up over my head and toss it aside.

Tim swipes at his mouth with hand, a raw sound escaping him. "Remember in the car when I said I wouldn't be able to keep my hands off you?"

"And yet," I say, "your hands are nowhere near me. Did you make a politician's promise, Timothy Holt?"

He destroys the small distance between the door and my bed and, with fluid grace, climbs onto it, his body looming over mine. I look up at him. God, he smells good. "No fucking way."

His lips crush mine as he presses me back onto the bed.

There's nothing shy or gentle about this kiss. Nor the way he's now touching me. One hand covers my breast, kneading it through the lace of my bra. My nipple pebbles and rubs against his palm, the abrasive contact sinking shards of sensations through me. His other hand cups the side of my face, his thumb sliding over my chin as his tongue slides over mine.

I spread my legs more and he nestles between them, and oh my God, he's so hard and close and *hard* and I arch beneath him because I want his hardness closer. I want it inside me, moving inside me, filling me.

A hungry whimper slips from me and he pulls his lips from mine, his hands growing still. "Too much?" Worry flickers in his eyes. "Tell me to slow down and I will."

"Not enough." I lock my legs around his waist and tangle

my fingers in his dark-auburn hair. "And don't you dare slow down."

A muscle bunches in his jaw and, before I can tell him to kiss me again, he lowers his head and captures my nipple with his mouth through my bra.

Oh. Yes.

He sucks, and I arch and whimper again, holding his head exactly where it is, even as I want to writhe in pleasure.

Oh. My. God. Yes!

His tongue flicks at my nipple before he sucks on it again, drawing it deeper into his mouth in pulses that drive me wild. I claw at his scalp and thrust my hips upward, aching for the solid length pressing to my sex. Denied to me by our jeans.

He releases my nipple with a pop, blows a soft cool stream of air on its wetness through my bra, and then moves his lips up over my chest, my throat, my jaw, my temple... "I want to be inside you," he whispers, pushing his erection gently against the junction of my thighs. The heat radiating from it turns my insides to liquid. Damn jeans. Keeping us apart.

"I'm totally okay with that," I reply, drawing him harder to me with my legs. And I am. I've never been one for one-night stands, not because I don't agree with them, I've just never met anyone I wanted to have one with. But Tim... I *really* want Tim to be inside me now.

Not just once. Not just for one night.

Lots and lots of times. Lots of lots of nights.

Which could be a problem, but right now, I don't care.

I'll take this moment, this night.

A raw groan rumbles deep in his chest and, before I know what he's doing, he's scrambling back off me and standing at the end of the bed.

He sucks in a choppy breath, his stare holding mine, and— with a playful grin—yanks his shirt up over his head.

My brain explodes. Oh baby.

There's no dad bod here: he clearly enjoys being healthy and fit. At least, that's what his sublime six pack and pecs tell me. I can't wait to lick them.

His hands move to his belt buckle, and I swallow, my mouth dry.

"Yes?" he asks, voice on the insanely sexy side of husky.

"Yes," I confirm, voice a scratchy breath. "Hell yes."

He chuckles and strips off his jeans as I squirm and wriggle out of mine.

"Beat you," he says, kicking his jeans aside.

I burst out laughing. He's wearing black *Star Wars* boxer briefs that have "These Aren't The Briefs You're Looking For" written all over them.

He grins, holds out his arms, looks down at himself and then back up at me. "I'm a closet geek."

"Impressive," I intone in my most Darth Vader-ish voice. "Most impressive."

His chest swells, and he shakes his head, climbing onto the end of the bed. "Fuck, I think I love you."

The statement is a growled chuckle, but it detonates in me something very dangerous. How amazing would it be to be loved by this man?

Before I can say something flippant—or foolish—*I think I love you too* comes to mind—he crawls towards me, a promise in his eyes.

He kisses me, and I kiss him back, my heart trying to hammer its way out of my chest as his hands trail their way around my back to my bra's clasp.

Dexterous fingers have it unclipped in a heartbeat and then it's not lace covering my breasts, but his hand. He cups one, gently at first, his lips still worshipping mine, as his other hand cups my jaw.

The tender sensation makes me melt, but right now, at this moment, I don't want tender.

I retrieve his other hand and place it over my other boob, arching into his palms as I nip his bottom lip.

He pulls away with a ragged breath, searching for something in my eyes, before, with a sound close to a growl, he presses me to my back on the bed, his body nestling between my thighs, his mouth finding my right nipple. He suckles deeply, cupping and squeezing my left breast as he does so.

My brain explodes again. My core does the same. Oh God, I think I'm going to orgasm already. Is that possible? Is it?

Do I care?

The world spins and swirls and I lose track of everything except Tim's mouth on my breast. The right one, the left. The right again. He teases my nipples, feasts on them, bites them, sucks on them again. Over and over.

Holy crap, it's more than good. The tight tension twisting in my core seems to consume me, replacing every sensation I know except pleasure.

"S...so good," I say, although I think I might be slurring it. I'm delirious with lust and need and pleasure.

And then he drags his lips from my breast, and kisses his way down my stomach, over my belly button, to my...oh boy.

He slips his fingers under the waistband of my underpants —thank God, I put my best pair on this morning and not my favourite ones with the saggy elastic—and, with a slight shift in his position, slips them down over my hips.

My breath catches. I grow motionless. This is really happening. This is really happening.

"Yes?" he asks again, his hands as still as I am.

"Yes," I confirm.

He removes my undies and, with another growling moan, dips his head and slowly parts my folds with his tongue.

And I'm done.

Game over.

I never want this to end.

He spreads my thighs a little wider with firm but gentle hands, his tongue finding and flicking my clit.

Over and over.

Until I'm drowning in pleasure and clawing at his hair, at the bedding underneath me, at his hair again.

His hands slip under my butt, and he lifts my hips upward a little, and before I know what I'm doing, I plant my feet on his shoulders and grind my sex to his mouth.

His hands turn fierce on my arse cheeks, his tongue the same on my clit.

I arch, driving my shoulders to the bed, as wave after wave of pleasure crashes over me.

And then, as his teeth nip my clit, he slips two fingers inside me and strokes my g-spot.

I erupt. Explode. Implode. Melt. Incinerate. Oh my God, it's almost an out of body experience. My orgasm rocks through me and I throw back my head, biting my lip to keep my cry silent.

Not because I don't want Tim to know I've come—I don't think there's any chance he could miss that—but because I don't want Gary coming in to investigate what's happening.

Instead, I let out a strangled whimper and rapid pants through my nose, my climax rolling and crashing through me until, just as Tim lifts his head from between my thighs, I slump into a boneless puddle of very-sated woman. "Oh... boy..."

His lips cruise the skin on my hip, my belly, my inner thigh, his hands feathering up over my ribs to my breasts. He brushes my nipples with his thumbs as he positions himself once again completely between my spread thighs. "You taste incredible."

For some reason his murmur brings a wave of heat to my cheeks. I open my eyes and prop myself up onto my elbows, looking at him. "Thank you."

I'm out of flippant and/or funny responses. I'm too shaken by what he's just done: the best orgasm of my life with only his mouth.

How do I regroup, recover from that?

His nostrils flare, and he levers back onto his heels, kneeling between my spread legs.

His cock is thick and erect and straining against his boxer briefs. I want to take it in my hands. I want to feel it fill my mouth. My—

In a fluid move, he's suddenly standing on my bed looking down at me, his hands on the waistband of his boxers.

I move before he can push them down, on my knees in front of him, snagging them with my fingers and dragging them down over his legs.

His cock springs free and I close my fingers around it. A tiny bead of moisture anoints its tip and, holding his gaze, I bend a little and lick it off.

His eyes roll back in his head, and he groans. Loudly.

"Shh," I half laugh, half protest, straightening at the waist to press my fingers to his lips and my breasts to his balls. "Gary will hear."

A wobbly chuckle falls from him. "Shall I close the door?"

"I'll close the door," I say softly, dancing my fingers down over his pecs, his amazing six pack, and up and down the length of his even more amazing cock. "You make yourself comfortable on the bed."

We move.

Keeping my footfalls soft, I hurry to my bedroom door and close it.

When I turn, Tim isn't on the bed. He's standing at the foot of it, frowning at something in his hand.

His wallet.

"Fuck," he mutters.

"What's wrong?" I cross back to him, a dark tension curling through my chest.

He looks at me, scowling. "I don't have a condom."

A relieved laugh bursts from me.

He blinks.

"Sorry." I hurry over to the top drawer in my dresser. "I just thought you were..." I pause, heat flooding my cheeks again. "Well, regretting what we'd just—"

He destroys the small space between us and silences me with a kiss that is at once savage and passionate, his hands cupping my face.

"No fucking way," he murmurs when he finally lifts his head from mine. "This, what we did, what we're going to do...it feels more right than anything I've done in a long, long time." He brushes his thumb over my bottom lip. "One hundred percent no regrets here." He pulls a face and any hope I have of not falling in love with him is shattered. "Okay, one regret. I regret not having a condom on me."

"I've got one," I say, pulling open my dresser's draw. "Only one, mind you."

Nestled amongst my underwear is a red satin drawstring bag; Kara's thirty-seventh birthday present to me.

I pull the bag out, tug it open and dump its contents onto the end of my bed.

Tim's eyebrows shoot up and his shoulders straighten. "Hey ho, there."

12

T *im*

I SCAN the array of items lying not-so-innocently on Chelsea's duvet, my cock growing harder by the second.

This is...unexpected.

There's two shiny red dice with various sexual positions printed on each side in gold, a pair of pink fluffy handcuffs, a black velvet eye mask, a black leather-wrapped stick I think is meant to be a small riding crop, a...a...God, I don't even *know* what the pink silicone ring with what looks like a pink silicone sea anemone attached to it is, a tube of lube—chocolate flavour—and a bright-purple square condom packet.

"It was a birthday present from my best friend," Chelsea says, indicating all the toys before plucking the condom from amongst them. She grins at me. "She called it my in-case-I-get-lucky care package."

My chest tightens at her lack of embarrassment at what

she'd upended on her bed. She's fucking amazing, and I think I want to spend the rest of my life with her.

Pulling in a slow breath, I gently take the condom packet from her fingers. "When you speak to your best friend next, please tell her I am eternally grateful for her gift choice. And you are very much about to *get lucky*."

Her grin stretches wider. I capture the playful happiness with my lips, and suddenly we're both on the bed again, lying on top of the sex toys, lips locked, limbs entwined.

I get lost kissing her. It's so easy. Her lips belong on mine. Her body does as well. Skin on skin, heartbeat to heartbeat, groin to groin...

With a groan, I pull back and, supporting my weight on my elbows, gaze down into her eyes. "I..."

She plucks the condom packet from my fingers, a gleam in her eyes.

Oh yeah.

I roll off her onto my back. Something fluffy stabs into my butt cheek—the handcuffs? I yank them out. Yep, the handcuffs—and then Chelsea is straddling my thighs.

Fuck. Me.

I toss the handcuffs aside—maybe later—and smooth my hands up her thighs to her hips, staring at her beautiful face as she slides the condom down the length of my shaft.

A shaky groan rumbles in my chest and she lifts her eyes to me. Her cheeks are flushed, her lips pink and swollen from our kissing. Strands of her hair have escaped her ponytail. She is the sexiest thing I have even seen.

"Yes?" she whispers. I know exactly what she's asking.

"Yes," I say. A million times yes.

Holding my gaze, she rises up onto her knees, shifts her position over me and slowly, slowly, impales herself on my cock.

Fuck.

Me.

I make a sound. I don't know what it is, but it makes her sex constrict tighter around my length and she lets out her own noise. It's raw and carnal. If you had to vocalise sex, the sound Chelsea just made would be it. Hungry blood rushes to my already rigid dick and I can't stop my fingers gripping her hips as I slam up into her.

"Oh yeah," she gasps.

And then there are no more words.

We just move together. In perfect rhythm. She rides my body, taking me deeper with every roll of her hips.

I'm mesmerised by the way she moves, the sublime strength in her soft curves. The sheen of sweat on her skin. The puckered perfection of her nipples.

I want to taste them. Now.

Sliding a hand up her spine, I draw her down to me, capturing one with my mouth, sucking on it with greedy force even as I thrust harder and faster into her.

She moans, her hands planted on either side of my head, her hips rolling back and forth, moving with my thrusts.

I worship her tits—they are utterly glorious—until she pulls back upright again, taking me deeper inside her.

I replace my mouth on her breasts with my hands, cupping them, kneading them. They fill each one, as if made for my palms, and it's too much. Her tight sex gripping and sliding up and down my cock, her full breasts bouncing in my hands, her ragged pants, her heavy-lidded, pleasure-filled gaze on mine...

It's too much. It's everything. It's perfect.

I try to warn her. Try to let her know I'm about to explode.

"Gonna... I'm gonna..." So much for grammar. "I'm gonna..."

A violent shudder rocks through her and she throws back

her head, her nails scoring my chest as her pussy constricts around my dick. "Holy crap," she cries. "*Yes!*"

I erupt, filling the condom.

We climax together, and slump in sated exhaustion together; Chelsea on my chest, her heart racing against mine, me still on my back, arms splayed.

I stare at her ceiling, head and body reeling.

"That was amazing," I murmur.

She lifts her head a little, enough to meet my eyes. "That's an understate—"

There's a scratching noise at her bedroom door.

Our stares lock.

"Gary," she said, pulling a face like a naughty child getting caught doing something naughty...and loving it. No regrets here. "Clearly I made too much noise."

With a soft chuckle, I brush the stray strands of her hair from her face. "Clearly."

She kisses me. "I'm hopping off," she declares. "Ready?"

A few seconds later, she's off me and the bed, heading for the door. "I'll deal with Gary, if you'll deal with..." she waves her hand at my groin. "Tissues by the bed. Waste bin in the bathroom."

And like that, she's gone. Naked. Without shame. Sexy as all sin.

I'm screwed.

There's no going back now.

I'm head over heels in love with her.

Scrambling off the bed, I hurry to the adjoining bathroom, deal with the condom—no leaks? Excellent—wash my hands and other parts of my body, and then walk back into her bedroom.

I look at the bed. At the toys on it.

We only had one condom and it's now gone, but that

doesn't mean I couldn't handcuff her to the bed and spend the next hour exploring every inch of her naked—

From the floor, my phone rings: Ellie's favourite song from *Encanto*. Which means Ellie is calling me.

Shit. Fatherly guilt wars with contented sexual pleasure inside me. No, I didn't forget I have a daughter waiting with my octogenarian neighbour for me to return, but I did...get lost in Chelsea's body for a while. I'll deal with the complicated, conflicting emotions later. Ellie's phone is for absolute emergencies only, which means something has gone wrong. God, I hope Mrs. Angelo is okay.

I hurry to where my jeans are a crumpled pile of denim on the floor, scoop them up, and snag my phone from the pocket.

Connect the call.

Press my phone to my ear. "Els? Everything okay?"

"Daddy!" Horrified excitement dances in her voice. "Wilbur pooed on Mrs. Angelo's living room rug!"

Well, crap.

Literally.

I know that rug. Her husband bought it for her a month before he passed away. And now my new dog has just taken a dump on it.

"How's Mrs. A?" I ask, picturing the scene. It's not a pretty image at all. "She mad?"

"Ummm..." Ellie pauses. "Maybe? Are you coming back soon?"

The uncertainty in her voice makes up my mind. "Yes," I answer, ramming my phone between my ear and shoulder so I can yank on my jeans.

Just as I start the awkward hopping dance, Chelsea enters the room, Gary at her feet. She stops and leans against the doorframe, watching me for a second. Gary sits beside her leg, doing the same.

At some point since leaving her bedroom, she's put on a big black AC/DC T-shirt that comes down to her mid-thigh. It's ridiculously sexy. I want to take it off her. So fucking badly.

"Going somewhere?" she mouths, a smile playing with her lips.

"Can Chelsea come back with you?" Ellie asks, the horror of Wilbur pooping on Mrs. Angelo replaced with the excitement of possibly seeing Chelsea again. "I like her."

My chest tightens. "I like her too."

Ellie hasn't "liked" anyone I interact with except Mrs. Angelo since Belinda's death. She hasn't been rude to anyone, just uninterested. I haven't even thought about dating since then, but any woman who's come to my home for whatever reason—be it in regards to my environmental work or my academic, or my new venture into the political life—has been met with indifference. She just didn't engage with them.

That she *likes* Chelsea...well, it's a big green flag. Are green flags a thing? I know red flags are. Whatever the opposite of a red flag is, that's what's waving above Chelsea's head right now.

Ellie likes her. I like her.

Wilbur likes her.

"I like her a lot," I continue, looking at her.

Chelsea's gaze holds mine. "I like you too," she mouths, bending a little to give Gary a soft stroke on his head. His tail wags.

"Can she come home with you then?" Ellie persists.

"Next time," I say. I need to process everything that's happened, and I can't do that with Chelsea in touching distance. There's been a monumental shift in...things, and I need to work out what happens next.

Dating? Getting to know each other? I mean, we've already skipped to the sex part, maybe dating isn't a thing anymore? Or is it? And if it isn't, what *is* next?

"Promise?" There's an equal mix of disappointment and hope in Ellie's question.

I've never promised her something I didn't one-hundred percent know I could deliver, and as much as I want to say *promise*, instead I say, "I'll be home soon. Tell Mrs. A I'm so sorry for what Wilbur did."

"Okay." She sighs dramatically into the phone, and then shouts, "Mrs. Angelo, Daddy says sorry."

Mrs. Angelo replies with something I can't make out.

"Hurry up, Daddy," Ellie says. "I love you."

She hangs up as I'm halfway through saying, "I love you right back." I'm looking at Chelsea when I say it and I'm pretty fucking certain the declaration wasn't limited to Ellie.

A monumental shift, indeed.

An unreadable expression flickers over Chelsea's face and she pushes herself from the doorframe and crosses to bed, dropping onto its end. "Wilbur okay?"

"Yeah," I say, a weird tension clamping around my chest. "Just took a dump on my neighbour's rug."

Confusion replaces her enigmatic expression. "He's not toilet trained?"

That weird tightness around my chest spreads to my gut, twisting into a knot. I have no fucking clue.

I should tell her right now I've only owned him for half a day. I should. But something stops me. We've just shared the most incredible sex and I'm not stupid enough not to think we partly got there because she believes I'm a dog person. And I am. I just didn't know I was until this morning. Until Wilbur. But if I admit Wilbur came into my life so I could have a reason to call her...

"The rug's special to Mrs. Angelo," I say, zipping up my fly. "I've gotta get back home. See if it's completely ruined."

"Mix half a tablespoon of dishwashing liquid with a tablespoon of white vinegar in two cups of warm water." She pats the bed beside her, and Gary leaps up and settles down against her thigh. "Use a clean cloth or sponge and blot the stain until it's gone."

"Thanks." I give her a wry smile. "This is the strangest post-coitus conversation I've ever had in my life."

Her laugh releases the knot in my gut, but not the tension around my chest. I remember that tension now. I experienced that same distinct sensation when I realised I was completely and irrevocably in love with Belinda twenty years ago.

"As far as post-coitus conversations go," she grinned, "it's typical for me."

A finger of jealousy shoots up my spine but I shove it aside, giving her a mocking narrowed-eyed inspection. "Oh, so you talk often of defecating dogs after sex, do you?"

"With all my partners," she answers, lips twitching.

I'm not going to ask her how many of those she's had because it's none of my business.

She reaches out and tugs me closer to her by the waistband of my jeans, tipping back her head to smile up at me as I bend down to her. "Well, if I'm being honest, only with the ones that count," she says softly, just before my lips find hers.

It takes more effort than it should to pull away. I do so only after picturing Mrs. Angelo's rug.

"I have to go," I murmur, nudging her forehead with mine gently before straightening. "Tomorrow night—"

"I'll meet you there," she says, giving Gary a slow pat.

I don't want to *meet* her there. I want to take her there. I want our dinner at Buckley's Chance to be a date so fucking much it hurts and picking her up from here and arriving there together would make it feel like that.

Instead, I nod. "Eight o'clock."

She smiles, and the tension around my chest is exquisite. "Eight o'clock. Now go attack the rug, Mr. Timothy Holt."

As far as dismissals go, it's gentle. But a dismissal all the same. Maybe she needs to process what's happened as well? I'm pretty certain neither of us planned to fall into bed with a complete stranger when we woke up this morning. Although to be fair, we stopped being complete strangers very quickly. Even before we made it to her bedroom.

I finish dressing and she walks me to the front door of her home. I pause, wanting to say something profound and significant. To let her know this is not normal for me. That this is special.

Instead, I drop into a crouch and give Gary a scratch behind his ears. "You're an awesome dog," I say. "I reckon you and Wilbur are going to get along really well."

I flick a glance up at Chelsea to see if she caught the probably not-so-subtle hint.

She's biting her bottom lip, watching me.

I slowly straighten. And kiss her.

She kisses me back.

"I'll see you tomorrow," I say, stepping backward through the door.

"Tomorrow."

"You're amazing," I say.

God, shut up, Tim. You'll scare her off.

"I know," she says, grinning.

"*Star Wars* reference?" I ask at the top of the porch steps, heart thumping a little faster. The famous line Han/Leia from the sci-fi film pops into my head: *Leia— I love you. Han— I know.*

She winks. "Say goodnight, wookie."

I chuckle. "Goodnight, wookie."

Yeah. I'm in love.

I'm ten minutes into my drive home when my phone rings. It takes me a few seconds to realise someone is calling me because my mind's roaring with a storm of questions and scenarios and what-ifs. Is Chelsea actually interested *in* a relationship? Is Ellie ready for me to *be* in a relationship? What does a relationship *mean* these days? When can I make love to Chelsea again? Is tomorrow night after dinner too soon? Could I use who I am, who my father is, to clear out the restaurant so I can make love to her there? On the table? Oh God, am I depraved?

Shaking away the enticing image of Chelsea splayed out naked on a white tablecloth, silverware and glassware and bread rolls scattered around her, my brain finally registers who's calling me.

I clench my jaw and stab accept. "Lyle, you've got some fucking explaining to do."

"Where are you?" he counters, uninterested in my ire. "I'm at your door and you're not home."

"Why are you at *my* door?" This guy. "And who gave you the right to go to *Chelsea's* door earlier today?"

"Please tell me you really didn't buy a dog?" he counters.

"Please tell me you didn't go to Chelsea's house in a misguided attempt to *scare* her off?" I hit back.

"Please tell me you were just trying to piss me off when you said you'd just bought a dog?"

So far, this conversation has been a slew of questions and not a single engaged response. The politician's way. Maybe I truly *am* cut out for the political profession? Following in Dad's footsteps?

"I *really* bought a dog," I snap.

He groans. Actually groans. "Dammit, Timothy, you can't just leap into this kind of thing."

I grind my teeth. "You can stick your focus groups up your arse, Lyle. I saw Wilbur. I fell in love with Wilbur. Period."

"Fine. I'll make it work. But if you tell me you're at Chelsea Parker's place..."

I saw Chelsea. I fell in love with Chelsea. Period.

"I'm not." I smile. "I've just left there."

"Are you *serious*?" he bursts out. I try not to snort with petty delight. "You're serious. Why? This is not conducive to your political path. At all. She's in a relationship, for Chrissake. She plays with dogs for a living. And she's...she's...fuck, she's public-school educated. Do you understand the optics here, Tim? Do you understand how this will sit with your voters?"

"She's a highly regarded and talented dog trainer." An icy anger snakes through me. "She's *not* in a relationship." Except maybe with me. "But we're having dinner together tomorrow night, so who knows what will happen after that. I don't give a fuck *where* she went to school. And as for these voters of mine you keep referring to: who are they, Lyle? I haven't even officially announced I am going into politics, let alone asked anyone to vote for me yet. And quite frankly, anyone who *wouldn't* vote for me because I interact with someone who didn't go to a private school is a fuckwit and I don't want their vote."

A beat of silence follows. And then, "Please God, tell me you haven't slept with her yet?"

"I'm done with this conversation," I say. "Whatever you think your job is, I'm terminating it. Thanks, but no thanks, Lyle."

"Timothy, wait."

"Tell Dad I said hi." I end the connection, furious.

What the hell does he have against Chelsea? She's the most honest, down-to-earth, what-you-see-is-what-you-get person I've ever met, a rarity in the circles I've spent most of my life in.

Who cares what Lyle thinks? Who cares what voters think?

All that matters is what I think, and what Ellie thinks—and Ellie is already at the "can Chelsea come?" stage.

In fact, so am I, and as crazy as it is, I'm going to tell her that tomorrow night.

I woke this morning thinking I was about to start a new direction in my life, and as it turns out, I am.

Just not the one I'd thought.

And I couldn't be happier.

Bring on dinner at Buckley's Chance.

I'm ready.

13

C *helsea*

ONLY TWO HOURS SLEEP, four in-home client visits, and two puppy-preschool classes all before lunchtime make for one very tired me.

I slump behind the wheel of Angus's Range Rover—my car is still parked in front of Tim's apartment complex—ignoring the buzzing from my handbag.

Marjory has called me three times this morning.

I've ignored every call. None were about Brutus. All were about when I was introducing her to Tim. It turns out, she somehow found out my car's location.

She's nothing if not persistent. Or maybe she's a tad stalkery?

Tim.

I sigh, slumping even more behind the wheel.

After Tim left last night I sat with Gary, trying to figure out what the hell had just happened.

I came to two possible options. One: I was dreaming and Tim and I *hadn't* had incredible, bone-melting sex, and two: it *wasn't* a dream, Tim and I were freakishly meant for each other, and we were going to have bone-melting sex often from now on.

Both were highly unrealistic and unlikely options.

I'd called Angus, told him my car had broken down, and asked if he would be able to help me with it tomorrow, i.e., today.

He'd asked how things had gone with my five o'clock meeting with Tim. I'd told him it'd gone well—no way was I giving him all the details. All the details opened up questions I didn't have answers for yet.

I could tell he wanted more info, but because he's an awesome brother he didn't ask. Yet.

Instead, he'd dropped his Range Rover around when he'd finished at the restaurant who knows when in the early hours of this morning. When I'd shuffled/lurched out into the kitchen this morning, I found his car keys and a note from him on the counter: *Don't crash it. I'll get it back tonight after your dinner with Holt.*

As far as brothers go, Angus is a keeper.

His Range Rover is also a keeper, but way out of my budget. It does, however, make for a comfortable place to have an existential crisis.

At some point, I'm going to have to respond to Marjory. She's too influential a client to ignore.

But the idea of pimping Tim out...

My stomach knots. Maybe I should tell him about her tonight.

Tonight.

I'm having dinner with Tim Holt tonight. The fact we're still having dinner after we've already had sex makes the actual meeting and talking over a meal more significant. If all that existed between us was lust, surely there'd be no need for dinner?

Sure, the whole original plan on my end was to get him to Buckley's Chance so I could meet him again, and somehow mention Marjory to him, somehow get them to interact, so she wouldn't influence my business into oblivion. And I guess I still need to do that, even if I don't want to, but now *this* dinner feels like a date.

Sex is one thing. Sex with Tim was mind-blowing and awesome and how the hell am I ever going to recover from it? But a *date* with Tim? A date plants a seed of hope for an impossible outcome: Tim Holt and Chelsea Parker in an actual relationship.

With a wry laugh, I press the button that starts Angus's Range Rover and head for home.

Saturday afternoons are Gary afternoons. Some serious Gary time will help alleviate the nerves and confusion gnawing away at me.

I hope.

"Hope." I snort. "There's that word a—"

My phone rings and I trail off. An unknown number.

Accepting the call, I put on my best Yes-you-*do*-want-me-to-help-train-your-dog voice. "Oh Behave Dog Training. Chelsea speaking."

"Ms. Parker," an unfamiliar and yet at the same time kind-of-familiar male voice says. "This is Robert Holt."

I blink. With how surreal my life has become in the last twenty-four hours, I shouldn't be surprised the ex-PM of Australia is calling me, but I am. "Seriously?"

He clears his throat. "I've been informed you've been spending some time with my son. Is this correct?"

My gut knots. Here we go again. "If it is?" Sure, he may be the ex-PM, but I never voted for him.

"Tim has a specific future mapped out, Ms. Parker," Robert Holt intones. God, his voice is the definition of stately. "I'm not sure if you are aware?"

A very specific future. What a weird life these people live. "Okay," I say. "So why are you calling me? I'm just his dog trainer."

Who had incredible sex with him and is having dinner with him tonight in what may or may not be a date.

"Hmmm," Robert Holt replies.

What the hell does *Hmmm* mean?

"Do you want something from me, Mr. Holt?" I legitimately have no clue how I'm meant to address a previous prime minister. "Or is this just a social chat?"

He chuckles.

I wasn't expecting that.

"I'm getting a good vibe from you, Ms. Parker."

"Thanks. I guess?" I shoot back. I'm so confused by this conversation.

"If Tim's life is to follow the path mapped out for him," Robert Holt says, "he will need people around him who aren't just sycophants. And his significant other will need to know how to handle unwelcome intrusions into their life." He chuckles again. "Like this one."

What the hell *is* this conversation?

"Sir." I shake my head, my grip on the steering wheel tight enough my knuckles are hurting. "I'm not sure my relationship with your son is what you think it—"

"He bought a dog yesterday after meeting you, Ms. Parker,"

Robert Holt interrupts, stately tone dialled up to eleven. "That tells me enough."

Something cold traces up my spine. Something hot and prickly crawls over my scalp.

He bought Wilbur *yesterday*?

Before I bumped into him on the footpath, he didn't own a dog, and then when I go to his house, he does?

Was he planning to get a dog? He had to be, right? Why didn't he mention he'd only owned Wilbur for the day? That's a pretty significant piece of information a dog trainer should know.

So why keep it a secret?

"Are you there, Ms. Parker?"

I blink at Robert Holt's question. "I'm sorry," I say, my head roaring. "I have to go. I'm driving, and it's my brother's car, and if I crash it, I'll have to mortgage my house to pay for the damages."

He laughs. Actually laughs.

Meanwhile, I can't comprehend what the hell is going on with my life.

"Those expensive European models will do that," he says, the smile in his voice wide and warm. If it wasn't for the weirdness of the moment, I'd probably smile back. "I am sure I will be meeting you soon, Ms. Parker. I look forward it. Until then, take care and drive safe."

He disconnects the call.

I blink again.

I can't fathom any of this. Did Robert Holt just call me? Did he imply I'm going to be Tim's significant other? Did Tim really buy a dog after meeting—

Those expensive European models.

Wait a minute. What did Robert Holt say again?

Those expensive European models.

I stiffen, my heart slamming up into my chest.

Those expensive European models.

How the hell does Robert Holt know Angus drives a Range Rover?

I shoot a look in the rear-view mirror. The car behind me—an old Toyota of some sort—is being driven by an elderly gentleman who looks like he's approaching seventy.

What did I think I was going to see? An ASIO agent driving a black SUV? A member of the Federal Police, lights flashing?

Those expensive European models.

Robert Holt knew what I was in. I don't know what that means but I don't think I like it. Or maybe I should be flattered. What the hell is going on?

And more to the point, did Tim buy a dog as an excuse to call me? Surely not?

Who would do that? Someone who truly wants a dog in their life? Or someone who just sees a dog as a means to an end? A way to get what they want in life? I can't believe he did it just to get in my pants; that would be absurd. So why? Is it just part of his mapped-out 'future plans'? A political move for his political ambitions?

That cold tension snakes up my spine again.

Whatever the reason, it's *no* reason to buy a dog.

Not. At. All.

It seems I was very wrong about Timothy Holt.

So what do I do now?

TIM

"ARE YOU OKAY, DADDY?"

I stop pacing around my bedroom—yep, I'm pacing—and

smile at Ellie. She's sitting in the middle of my bed. Wilbur is sitting on her lap. Beside them both is Lord Byron. The bear looks free of dog slobber so evidently Wilbur doesn't care about it anymore. A win. Yay.

"I'm nervous." I tug at the collar of my shirt and tie.

Ellie giggles, mischief twinkling in her eyes. "About going on a date with Chelsea."

I told Ellie I was going out to dinner with Chelsea tonight. I didn't tell her it was a date. She decided it was a date. Who am I to tell her she's wrong? She likes Chelsea and is very excited about the idea of me eating dinner with her. Besides, maybe this dinner *is* a date? Maybe?

Damn it, I wish I'd been able to get a hold of Chelsea this afternoon. I'd tried. I'd called her to see if I could convince her to let me pick her up—date!—but she didn't answer. No doubt helping someone else with their dog.

"Yes." I yank my tie off and chuck it away. A tie? Really? I rarely do ties. "I'm nervous about going to dinner with Chelsea."

Ellie frowns. "Why?" She giggles again. "Are you nervous about the kissing?"

I stop myself from choking on my own breath. Just.

More giggles from the bed. "Daddy's going to kiss Chelsea," Ellie whispers loudly into Wilbur's ear. Wilbur's stubby tail thumps on the duvet: *thud, thud, thud*, before he licks her face.

"Now who's getting kisses?" I chuckle, raking my hands through my hair.

"Me!" She pulls Wilbur into a hug. Wilbur doesn't seem to mind at all, happily licking at her face again. For a dog who came close to ruining Mrs. Angelo's cherished rug yesterday, he's pretty chill.

Mrs. Angelo is also very chill about the rug. Possibly

because I paid to have it and the rest of her apartment's flooring professionally cleaned this morning.

"Poppy said I can bring Wilbur tonight," Ellie informs me.

"No, he didn't," I say. Maybe I should rethink the jeans I'm wearing. Are jeans too casual for Buckley's Chance? Maybe? They *are* ethically and sustainably produced though. Okay, if Colin doesn't get here soon to collect Ellie, I'm going to be late. Did I put on deodorant? Jesus, brain, stop!

"Yes, he did," Ellie insists.

"Poppy doesn't like dogs." The jeans are staying. But maybe I should change my Chuck All-Stars for a pair of R.M. Williams boots?

"Poppy will love Wilbur." Chelsea hugs Wilbur tighter as if the notion of the great Robert Holt not being a dog fan might wound him. "When he was telling me what we're going to do tonight while you're kissing Chelsea, he said we can take Wilbur on Matilda."

I picture Wilbur on Dad's superyacht. Then I picture myself kissing Chelsea.

My heart quickens, but I focus on the Wilbur-on-Dad's boat issue. What's Dad's game? He *doesn't* like dogs. And when I'd told him this morning that, yes, I *had* bought a dog, he'd sounded less than impressed. Now he's inviting Wilbur into his home?

I shoot Wilbur a quick look. Wilbur wags his tail. "Mrs. Angelo offered to babysit Wilbur tonight."

Problematic as my dubious trust in my father in this particular instance may be, I'll feel better with Wilbur *not* on Dad's boat. Too easy for a three-legged dog to accidentally fall overboard into the dark Sydney Harbour waters, I think.

Ellie isn't impressed with me. She pouts, hugs Wilbur again, and then crawls off the bed. "Have fun kissing Chelsea," she mumbles, dragging her feet out of my room.

"Els," I call. Wilbur looks at me, and then bounds after Ellie. I chuckle. I know where his loyalties lie.

The fact Wilbur and Ellie clearly love each other already makes me smile. I couldn't be happier.

Everything about bringing Wilbur into my life, our life, is perfect. Ellie and Wilbur, me and Chelsea...

Nerves twist in my gut and I drag my hands through my hair again. "It's going to be okay, Holt," I mutter, heading from my bedroom. "Dinner is going to be—"

The door buzzer lets me know Colin has arrived.

Wilbur's excited barking emphasises the fact. As does Ellie's laughs as she and the dog hurry for the door.

I reach it at the same time they do. "Wilbur, sit."

He does. A perfect three-legged sit, looking up at me, ears pricked, tail swooshing side to side on the polished floorboards.

A grin stretches across my face. I am going to kiss the hell out of Chelsea when I see her.

"Are you *sure* Wilbur can't come with me?" Ellie asks, her sleep-over-at-Poppy's-place backpack already on her shoulder as I turn the doorknob. Lord Bryon is peeking out from behind the open zipper, judging me.

"How 'bout you, me, Chelsea, and Wilbur all go to Poppy's house next weekend for lunch?" I offer. That way I get to monitor Dad around my new dog, and...well, get to introduce Chelsea to him.

You don't think you're jumping the gun somewhat, Tim? What if Chelsea's not ready to meet family by then?

I ignore the internal rebuke and open the door.

Colin is there. Along with Mrs. Angelo.

"Colin!" Ellie beams at Dad's driver. "I've got a dog. His name is Wilbur. He's got three legs!"

"I know." Colin produces a broad smile, and a milkshake from behind his back. "And I've got a milkshake."

Ellie laughs, takes the usual treat/bribe, and grins up at me. Daring me to take it from her.

"Not my problem tonight." I shrug. "Poppy's the one dealing with your sugar rush." I flick Colin a smirk. "And a certain driver knows that."

"And *I've* got a Schmackos." Mrs. Angelo waves a brown, floppy stick of something at Wilbur. Bouncing to his feet, Wilbur wags his tail. Pointed humour dances in the look Mrs. Angelo gives me. "And a bucket and sponge. Just in case."

"Enjoy your date, Daddy," Ellie exclaims, wrapping my legs in a hug. "And the kissing."

Mrs. Angelo arches an eyebrow at me. Okay, I'm going to be in for an interrogation tomorrow morning.

Colin clears his throat and looks at the ceiling. "Ready, Miss Holt?"

"Ready, Wilbur?" Mrs. Angelo asks, a dog leash suddenly in her hand.

And just like that, I'm sans one child and one three-legged dog.

Excitement and nerves smash into me. Oh boy. Here we go. In forty minutes, I'll be having dinner with Chelsea. Jesus, why am I so nervous?

You know this is a moment. A significant moment.

More significant than officially announcing my political career intentions? 'Cause I sure as hell didn't feel nerves like this yesterday morning leading up to and during my television appearance.

Maybe.

Yeah, definitely.

Wow.

I suck in a slow breath. Let's do—

My phone buzzes with an incoming message, and my heart slams up into my throat. Chelsea?

Yanking it from my pocket, I stare at the screen and the text message on it.

Not Chelsea.

Lyle.

Chelsea Parker is pimping you out to her clients. In return they will recommend her business on social media. She's cashing in on who you are, Timothy. Just thought you should know.

Something tight knots in my gut. Frowning, I read the message again. No. This is bullshit. I don't believe—

Another message from Lyle, this one with a link to an Instagram post: **See?**

The knot in my gut tightens. The Instagram profile is vaguely familiar. Someone called...

"Marjory_With_A_Why." Now I remember. This was one of the Instagram accounts posting about Chelsea knocking me off my feet yesterday morning. One of the ones with an embarrassing Tim Holt hashtag.

I turn my attention to the post itself and the tight knot in my gut turns into a sour ball. A sinking, sour ball.

It's an image of Marjory holding up a photo of me, making goo-goo eyes at it. And across the image, in bright-red comic sans are the words *Guess Who I'm Meeting Soon? Thank you @OhBehaveDogTraining. Love you, Chels!*

What. The. Fuck?

14

C helsea

"WHY DO you look like you're about to go to the dentist?"

Ignoring Angus's confused question, I chew on my thumbnail, staring into Buckley's Chance's dining area from the private outside deck.

The night is beautiful; the lights of the city reflect on the calm Sydney Harbour waters, boats and yachts glide over its surface, the promenade beside the restaurant is full of laughing pedestrians enjoying the evening, and somewhere further along the walkway a live band plays Blackthorne and Synergy covers with so much talent I can almost believe it's Nick or Josh Blackthorne singing themselves.

I'm wearing the dusky-pink satin shift dress I bought for Kara's wedding last year and the only stilettoes I own. My hair is perfect, my boobs are behaving themselves, and because I haven't eaten a damn thing since my conversation with Robert

Holt this morning, there's not a hint of bloat. I've got the stomach I always want.

I look amazing. I should be floating. I'm having dinner at Sydney's most exclusive, awarded restaurant, I'm looking good, and I'm about to share a table for two with one of the hottest guys in the country. Maybe the planet.

A guy who quite possibly bought a dog as an excuse to call me.

Maybe some would be flattered. Maybe I should be, but the fact he didn't tell me he'd only owned Wilbur for half a day...

"Oi!" Angus clicks his fingers in front of my face and, still chewing on my thumbnail, I glare at him.

He frowns. "Am I missing something?"

I open my mouth to tell him what's on my mind, and snap it shut again.

Tim is standing with the restaurant's maître d', looking at me.

My heart slams into my throat. God, he is so freaking gorgeous. Faded denim jeans, a loose black shirt—rolled up at the sleeves. Are you freaking kidding me?—and open at the neck enough to show off just a tease of his chest at the base of his throat. His hair looks a tousled mess. His jaw is shaded with a ginger five o'clock stubble.

I want to walk over there, snake my arms around his neck, and kiss him for everyone to see.

I want to know why he bought Wilbur and why he didn't tell me he'd only just done so.

"Okay, sis." Angus is suddenly at my side. "Let's get you and Holt started."

Oh boy, we got started yesterday. But maybe we've already finished?

"Okay," I whisper. Tim's watching me, an unreadable

expression on his face. I kissed that face only twenty-four hours ago.

Angus opens the heavy glass door and I walk through it. Follow him to the table he'd set aside for Tim and me. An invisible weight tells me Tim is watching. I'm not stupid enough to try to up my sexy-walk game.

But why would I want to? He's an irresponsible dog owner.

Sinking into the plush chair at my table, I draw in a shaky breath and watch Angus drape a pristine white napkin over my lap. "Have fun," he murmurs under his breath as one of his staff leads Tim over to us.

He's gone by the time Tim sits in the chair on the other side of the table.

We're given the menus and asked if we want anything to drink while deciding on our meals.

We both say *water*. Almost at the same time.

Oh boy. Something isn't right. I'm angry at him, but he doesn't know that yet. So why does *he* look angry? Is he upset I didn't answer his calls this afternoon? I was busy. Saturday afternoons are Gary afternoons, after all. Or maybe he's regretting what happened between us.

God, I am so not good at this human interaction thing. Maybe Roger *was* correct when he said I was hopeless at people relationships?

Relationship? Ha. You're not in a relationship. You're pissed at Tim because he bought a dog! You're broken.

Our waitress flicks a look back and forth between us and then hurries away.

We're alone. As much as you can be in a busy restaurant.

His jaw knots.

"Hi," I say. I need to say something. The tension in unbearable. And I think people are looking.

"You know the chef?" he asks without saying *hi* back.

Not how I thought he'd join the conversation. "He's my brother."

His jaw knots even more. Something flickers in his eyes. As if he doesn't like the answer.

"Half brother," I clarify. "We had the same dad."

There goes the knot in the jaw again. "Did you know he offered me this table, this dinner, tonight?"

Umm...crap.

"Who's Marjory_With_A_Why?" he asks before I can reply.

I blink. "What?"

"Marjory_With_A_Why." He narrows his eyes. There's an edge to his voice, a tiredness. "She's an Instagram influencer."

Oh God, what's Marjory done? I ignored her calls and messages all day. If I didn't, I would have probably told her to sod off. Not good for my business.

"Marjory Whitton," I say, my pulse pounding in my ears. "She's one of my clients. I'm helping her with her Rottie, Brutus." I swallow. "Why?"

He pulls his phone from his hip pocket, taps his thumb on its screen a few times and slides it across the table, and I'm confronted with an image of Marjory holding a photo of Tim.

My stomach sinks. Oh my God, Marjory! Are you freaking kidding me?

"I didn't promise her this." I shake my head. His frown expresses doubt. "I didn't. She saw all the posts about our... interaction yesterday morning and started harassing me about introducing you to her. I tried to tell her I didn't know you."

"But you do now."

Something cold races up my spine. He's angry. Very angry.

"I do. Now."

Once again, his jaw knots. "And she posted this—" he taps his phone—"about an hour ago. So, when are we meeting her? Or is she joining us for dinner?"

"I had nothing to do with this, Tim." My head is roaring. "I promise. I haven't spoken to her since yesterday morning after we collided on the footpath. I wouldn't do anything like this to you. To anyone."

"Not even to help your business?"

My stomach knots.

His eyes narrow. "Not even to get her to recommend your business to all her followers?"

This is exactly what I'd thought of doing. Hell, I'd even roped Angus in to helping me. Well, after Lyle insulted me, Angus had decided to go full-on big-brother mode, but I hadn't stopped him. We're here, at his restaurant, after all.

"So your brother calls me out of the blue," Tim says, stare locked on mine, "and offers me a table at his restaurant. What was the plan? Were you going to show up here anyway? With Marjory Whitton?"

"No." It wasn't the plan. "I was going to be sitting at the table next to you. Alone." I let out a wry, weak laugh. "An *oh, look who else is here* moment."

He closes his eyes, shoulders slumping. A little.

"But it wasn't for Marjory's benefit," I say. I feel sick. Here I was, all angry at him for buying a dog and meanwhile, I've been running around behaving like a stalker. Who has the right to be angry here? It's not me.

Steel seems to glint in his eyes. "No?"

"It was for mine." The truth is damning, but I can't lie. "I wanted to meet you again. I wanted to...to have you meet me again. I mean, let's be serious here, you and I don't move in the same circles, we don't even *exist* in the same circles—there's a reason Lyle came to my home to tell me you're off-limits—but I just wanted one more moment of talking to you. Seeing you. So Angus, God love him, decided to help. I thought we'd maybe exchange a few words, and in my little fantasy you'd think, *hey, I like this girl. We've got a connection. Maybe we could do coffee one day*. That was it." I sigh. "But then you actually called me and asked me to dinner here."

He draws in a swift breath.

I study him. "You called and asked me to have dinner with you, and I got excited. And then you said it was so we could discuss dog training."

His jaw knots once more, and he looks away from me for a split second.

"For a dog you'd only just bought," I say, a prickling heat crawling over me.

He shifts on his seat.

I frown. "Wilbur. He's an awesome doggo. You led me to believe you'd owned Wilbur for a while. In fact, every time I tried to get information that would help with his training about how long you'd had him for, you dodged those questions." Like a politician. "Why? Why didn't you want me know you'd only just bought him?"

He holds my stare.

My heart hammers. There's no sound in the room—just the roaring of my blood in my ears and Tim's shaky breath. "Why, Tim?"

"I came here angry at you," I confess, fiddling with the napkin on my lap. "Your father rang me—"

His eyebrows shoot up. "He what?"

"He called me earlier today. Told me I must be pretty special to make you suddenly buy a dog. Told me you'd bought a dog yesterday morning after we met each other for the first time. Is that right?"

His Adam's apple jerks up and down his throat.

"Buying a dog is lifelong commitment, Tim. A life-changing decision. Not a knee-jerk one. You're taking responsibility for another living thing's existence. And Wilbur...what kind of life did Wilbur have before you plucked him out of the shelter? He's aching for love and a forever home, and what happens when you realise caring for a three-legged dog—one who's probably been abused or at least neglected and rejected —isn't easy? What do you do then? Just take him back to the shelter?"

He shakes his head, but I'm already seeing Wilbur—and countless dogs like Wilbur—back in a cold concrete enclosure. I'm angry again. For Wilbur. For all the dogs in the world denied love and comfort and a home. For all the dogs bought on a whim, only to be cast aside and abandoned.

"That's not..." He trails off, frowning. "Well, maybe... There were a lot of forces at work, Chelsea. A lot."

I throw up my hands. "A lot? For Pete's sake, if it was so you could talk to me, you could have just freaking called. Said *Hi, remember me? You knocked me on my arse today on the footpath. Would you like to maybe go for coffee one day?* Or had Lyle convinced you I was just a social-climbing nobody."

There goes that knot in his jaw again. "I didn't listen to a word Lyle said about you. In fact, Lyle is partly responsible for me getting Wilbur. He was so adamant I get some kind of designer mutt when I kept telling him over and over that I didn't *want* a dog. So I..."

He trails off again, staring at me.

My stomach knots again. "You've just realised what you said, right?"

"It's not..." He claws his hands through his hair. "It's not... That's not... Ah, fuck," he ends on a mutter.

Drawing in a slow, deep breath, I gently push his phone back across the table to him and, with a just-as-gentle smile, rise to my feet. "It was incredible meeting you, Tim. I will never forget it. Good luck with your political career."

He jolts to his feet. "Chelsea, wait."

I swallow the lump in my throat, looking at him as I sling my handbag over my shoulder. "And when you decide Wilbur isn't for you... Well, give me a call. I think he and Gary will love each other."

I turn and walk out of Buckley's Chance.

I know people are watching me. I'm pretty certain some of them are surreptitiously filming my exit on their phones. I don't care. I'll explain everything to Angus later. Apologise if it has any kind of negative impact on his restaurant.

The long and short of it is, Tim and I? We have no chance. Even if we both hadn't manipulated and lied by omission to each other from the beginning, he's quite likely the future prime minister of Australia, and I'm a dog trainer with a dead father who was an abusive alcoholic when he was alive.

I'm on the esplanade, opening my Uber app, blinking like a mad woman so I don't burst out crying, when a hand touches my elbow.

Tim stands there, his face impossible to read. "I like you a lot, Chelsea. More than it's logically possible, given I've only just really met you, but I don't care. And yes, I bought Wilbur so I could call you, get to know you."

A hot lump forms in my throat and I bite my lips. "Thank you," I say, my voice a husky croak. "But that's not why someone should get a dog."

His Adam's apple jerks up and down his throat again.

I give him a wobbly smile. "It was fun, Tim. While it lasted."

He opens his mouth and closes it.

Before I can do something silly like throw myself against his body and tell him I don't care why he bought Wilbur, I turn and hurry away, the sweeping white arcs of the Opera House mocking my misery with their breathtaking beauty.

Stupid opera house.

I send Angus a text as I'm waiting for my ride to arrive:

It didn't pan out. But thank you for being an incredible brother.

He texts back almost immediately.

He's still here. Standing in the private section of the deck. Looking out at the view. He looks miserable. What happened?

I grimace. **I'll tell you later,** I text back. **Promise.**

My phone buzzes. **Sure you don't want to come back?**

No, I'm not sure, I tap out. **But I'm not.**

You going to be okay? Angus asks.

Am I? I've spent my life, from as far back as I can remember, caring for dogs, fostering them when they'd been abandoned and rejected, volunteering at shelters, studying dog psychology and behaviour, training them. I've seen too many unwanted dogs go through the system. Too many dogs lose their faith in mankind. My gut tells me what Tim did was wrong. So wrong. But my heart...

Maybe, I text back. **Ask me tomorrow**.

Angus sends back a thumbs-up emoji, a crazy-face emoji, and a steak emoji. Because he's Angus.

I chuckle, throat still thick, and open my app to track my ride's arrival.

It takes me forever to get home. Longer than it should. I rarely come into Sydney City at night, even less so on a Saturday night. The traffic is ridiculous. And my driver is just as clueless about it as I am. Plus I made the mistake of getting a group share, which goes just as well as you can imagine. On the plus side, I'm completely distracted the whole way home by the two cosplayers who join the ride a few minutes after I get in. Who knew I was going to be in a car with a gender-bent Wonder Woman—biggest biceps I've seen—and an Asian Aquaman.

They wave me off with extravagant blown kisses as they

pull away from the kerb outside my home, heading to who knows where—but wherever it is, I bet the party is wild.

I stand in the dark, laughing for a moment, even as my stomach grumbles. I'm hungry. I may be heartbroken, but I'm hungry. Vegemite on toast, here I come. Not quite as good as what Angus would have made for me, but still, a deluded, stubborn, probably irrational girl's gotta eat.

My key has just slid into the front door lock when I hear a car door slam shut behind me.

"Chelsea!"

My breath catches as Tim's shout cuts through the night, and I turn around.

He's standing beside the driver's door of his Volvo on the other side of the road. His hair's a dishevelled mess. Wilbur is sticking his head out the back passage window, tongue lolling. He barks, and I can't stop my smile at how happy the sound is.

"Chelsea," Tim calls again, giving Wilbur's head a stroke. "I stuffed up. I did. I know that."

My heart racing like a hyperactive greyhound, I let out a sigh.

He pats Wilbur again, checks the dark road both ways, and jogs across to my side.

I don't move. I don't know what to do, what to feel.

Yes, you do.

But I can't move. This is too big, and my emotions are already so messed up.

No, they're not.

He stops in front of me, chest heaving. "I stuffed up," he repeats. Anguish cuts the words and my stomach clenches. "I know you don't buy a dog to meet a girl, but when I met you… everything I knew got knocked off kilter. I thought I knew exactly where I was going with my life, exactly what my future held, and then you knocked me on my arse and…" A wry smile tugs at his lips and he shrugs. "And my brain—an organ I'm usually pretty proud of—let me down."

I swallow. Behind him, Wilbur barks from the backseat.

"But I don't regret getting Wilbur at all." He shakes his head, and the love that fills his face... Yep, there goes my heart again, slamming into my throat. "And I know it's going to be hard, but I don't care. Because he's fucking awesome, and I'm going to be there for him forever."

I look up at him, slide my gaze to Wilbur—half hanging out the back window—and back to Tim. "Did you seriously go back to your place to get Wilbur? To come here?"

He shakes his head. "No. I seriously got Colin to go get Wilbur and meet me here."

I blink.

"Colin's parked just down there." He points down the road and I can see a black SUV lurking in the darkness a few houses away. From behind the wheel, a dark shape waves at me. I raise my hand and wave back before I realise what I'm doing. "And I'm telling you this because I'm not going to keep things from you again. Ever."

I look back at him.

He steps closer to me, his gaze holding mine. "Wilbur showed me that love at first sight is one-hundred percent real. It's a legit feeling. The moment I saw him in the shelter, something changed inside me. Something wonderful. Something I didn't realise I wanted to change until it did. I recognised that sensation because the moment I saw *you*, on the street, standing over me with an empty pineapple juice bottle in your hand," he lifts his hand and gently brushes his thumb along my jaw, "something changed inside me as well. Something I hadn't realise I wanted to change changed."

His thumb brushes my jaw again. My bottom lip. I want to turn my face into that tender caress so freaking much. Instead,

I stare up at him. Balancing on a terrifying, wonderful precipice.

"Please," he whispers, "give me a chance. Give me and Ellie and Wilbur a chance."

I swallow. I'm thrumming. My heart is pounding. "Tim…"

He dips his head closer to mine. "I thought I wanted to be the prime minister, but I realise now, that's not enough."

"It's not?" I whisper.

He shakes his head, cupping my face with both hands. "I want a future with you. Being PM is a distant second."

"What if the voters don't like me?" How do I even have breath to say the words?

"How could they *not* like you?" he whispers back, his forehead almost brushing mine. "You're fucking amaz—"

I shut him up with a kiss.

He grabs my arse and kisses me back.

Wilbur barks from the car.

He pulls away, a soft chuckle falling from him. "So, shall we introduce Wilbur to Gary?"

"Sure." I grin, smooth my hands up his back, and bury my fingers in his hair. "But first…" I pull him down to me.

There's some serious kissing to be done.

Right here. Right now. On my front porch for all the world to see.

EPILOGUE

*S*ix months later

TIM

"ELLIE, we are going to be late!" I call over my shoulder, tossing Lord Byron into her bedroom.

A seismic rumble vibrates through the hallway floor and up into my legs, just as Ellie, Wilbur, and Gary come barrelling past me.

"Ellie!"

"I'm cleaning my teeth, Daddy!" She disappears into the bathroom, Wilbur and Gary joining her.

I roll my eyes.

"Have *you* cleaned *your* teeth?" Chelsea's arms snake around my waist and I twist in her embrace, flashing her my pearly whites.

She laughs. I kiss her.

I kiss her a lot. First thing in the morning, last thing at night. When I'm making dinner. When she's making dinner. I even kissed her while she was sitting on the loo the other morning.

That kiss turned into a bit of a laughing fest but sometimes, laughing kisses are the best kisses.

"We *are* going to be late," she says, pulling away and giving my chest a soft shove. "It'll take us at least thirty minutes to get to the studio. Hurry up."

I grimace, snag her wrists as she goes to walk away, and yank her back to my body. "The interview can wait," I growl, cupping her incredible butt with my hands. "I want to make love to your mouth with my mouth for a while."

She snorts, but yeah, here we go, up onto tiptoe, her lips almost on mine, and then she's skipping backward, grinning. "Did you hear that, Colin?" she calls, mischief in her eyes as she watches me.

Colin's here? Already? He's five minutes early.

"Unfortunately," the sound of Colin's voice wafts from the living room, "yes."

I narrow my eyes and shake my head. "You're going to pay for that," I mouth at her as she continues to shimmy backward away from me.

She blows me a kiss before pivoting on her heel and strutting down the hallway. Our new home, a self-sustained, off-the-grid, powered-by-renewables four-bedroom on the waterfront at Point Piper, has a hallway long enough to have sprint races in. I know: Ellie, Wilbur, and Gary do so every day.

"Hurry up," Chelsea tosses over her shoulder as she reaches our bedroom door. "There's a whole TV audience of potential voters waiting to be charmed by you this morning, Federal Minister for the Environment."

"By *us*," I call, still liking the sound of my newly appointed political title. It's a step. The first of many to changing the country, and hopefully, the world. "By you, me, Ellie, Gary, *and* Wilbur."

"By *you*, Mr. Holt," she says, pointing at me. "Today, we're just window-dressing."

I smile. "As long as *you're* charmed, *Mrs.* Holt, who cares about anyone else."

She arches an eyebrow at me, mischief twinkling in her eyes. "I'm going to tell Lyle you said that."

I laugh.

Fuck, I love her.

WANT MORE OF ANGUS?

Chelsea's amazing brother, Angus, can be found getting his own HEA in **Hot Aussie Night** (*The De Luca Sisters*, Book Two)

The *De Luca Sisters* is a trilogy starring three American triplets, Bria, Elisa, and Zeta, and the Aussie men who fall in love with them.

It's all insta-love, HEAs, and steamy sensuality.

Are you ready?

The De Luca Sisters Trilogy

Along Came An Aussie

Hot Aussie Night

Aussie Actually

Available Now in eBook

The De Luca Sister Collection also available in print paperback.

THANK YOU

If you enjoyed **Who's A Good Boy?**, follow Lexxie on Bookbub for pre-order, sales and new-release alerts. Sign-up for her newsletter, the Lexxicon to receive a free copy of her (erotic) paranormal short story, **The Cavern**, plus never miss out on exciting announcements and giveaways!

ABOUT LEXXIE COUPER

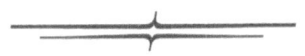

Lexxie writes fun-with-feels romances. She lives with a manic rescue dog, a self-absorbed rescue cat, a very patient husband not rescued from anything, and two strong-willed teenage daughters who will one day rule the world.

Lexxie lives by two simple rules – measure your success not by how much money you have, but by how often you laugh, and always try everything at least once. As a consequence, she's laughed her way through many an eyebrow raising adventure. You can find details of her writing at
www.LexxieCouper.com

MORE ROMANCE FROM LEXXIE COUPER...

The Always Series

Unconditional
Unforgettable
Undeniable

The Outback Skies Series

Bound to You
Breathless for You
Burn for You
Bare for You
Better with You

The Heart of Fame Series

Love's Rhythm
Muscle for Hire
Guarded Desires
Steady Beat
Lead Me On
Blame it on the Bass
Getting Played
Blackthorne

Stimulated

Blowing It Off

Revving It Up
Switching It On
Rubbing It Out
Pinning It Down

The De Luca Sisters Trilogy

Along Came An Aussie
Hot Aussie Night
Aussie Actually

Heart of Fame: Stage Right

Compliance
A Single Knight
Balls Up
Lust's Rhythm

Dangerous Desire

The Bad Boy Next Door
The Good Girl in My Bed
The Bad Boy in Cuffs
The Good Girl in Trouble

www.ingramcontent.com/pod-product-compliance
Lightning Source LLC
Chambersburg PA
CBHW020010140726
47904CB00018B/2208